Their After

LIFE

by Alan Updyke

The earth shakes violently and the struggle of their after lives becomes the ultimate test.

The Contemporary Christian series

REVELATION

4. Realize the life chosen.

"And I beheld when he had opened the sixth seal, and, lo, there was a great earthquake;" **(Rev 6:12)**

Their After Life

It is the most haunting question of all time. Religion has failed to give us an adequate answer.

They were fraternal twins and knew each other intimately. Some said they were telepathic. Everyone believed that their union was unbreakable. But life drove them apart. This is their story.

But the tale of Darren and Deidra Daniels as eloquently told in "**Their After Life**," is more than fiction - it is also an accounting of this age. Historical facts noted in *bold* lettering document the influence of these events upon the book's main characters. And as the fictional story moves forward in time, there is a prediction for our future.

It is the mysterious contents of a small wooden box preserved by their great grandfather who lived during the Civil War that affected more than just the twins. It has the power to change all of America.

Now you must discern is meaning.

Hence the question returns. Life or death - heaven or hell: based on the evidence of your life, how will you plea?

And with the moral of the story you will gain the knowledge needed to understand the ultimate test. It is coming.

Contents: the novel at a glance. It's a book with insight for the future, based on historical facts and an interpretation of prophetic writings.

Foreword

I looked at my 10-year-old son and wondered with concern what the future holds for him. I was simultaneously wrestling with mine, in the context of my dismal present financial failure.

So, I asked my son if he can suggest a title for a new book. He's a fifth grader that exudes confidence. Sometimes it's more than I understand, and by it can feel challenged. I try not to humiliate this boy, but as the supervising adult I often feel humbled by him. There should be no contest between us. My role is to help him become his very best.

But it seems that he has no motivation. I keep telling myself that it will come in time, that it's a simple matter of maturity.

"Sure Dad," he gives me a quick glance over the top of his iPad as he continues to play a video game.

"Well?" I wait patiently.

"Hell's Revenge," he answers as the game action slows, allowing him to divert some of his attention my way.

In introduction, let me say that I am a writer, and have been my entire life. My career led to a dead-end without reward or recognition. I owned and operated a family business, and published a community newspaper. It closed one year before its 50th anniversary. I was left holding the proverbial bag, and it was full of debt. There was no acknowledgement of the paper's accomplishments, of the many, many years, five decades of publishing – some 2,500 editions. Somehow their influence in documenting and shaping the course of events that changed our community was immediately cancelled, erased by the closure. It was forty-nine years, two generations, and nearly golden – but naturally, in the end there was no spirit of celebration in its demise.

It's the way of newspapers today, so I'm told in sympathetic reassurance.

Having filed for an early retirement I did what a writer does, I wrote my first novel, and then, my second.

We seem to put what drives us into two opposing categories: that which we can control, and that which controls us. Honestly, I'm not sure which way to label my obsession with writing; however, I'm reluctant to call it a disease.

Then again, I most likely am stricken. And aren't we all? I am well aware of my faltering physical prowess, and now giving increasing concern to my mortality. I ponder my spiritual life. Healthy or ailing? Death is the disease of immortality, or is it?

The trees around me are dying. There seems to be a pestilence in nature. The smallest, most insignificant insects are delivering the most dreadful and damaging diseases to mankind. It seems that the supply of clean air and water is minimal, and running low. Terrorists hate us. Danger constantly looms everywhere.

What kind of a world is my son growing into?

Obviously, I have too much idle time on my hands.

"What do you mean?" I ask, surprised at his title suggestion and wondering at its meaning.

"Okay," my boy answers. "The story goes like this... Satan creates monsters, monsters of all kinds, like zombies, to attack the world."

He pauses and presses the game controller with his thumbs as the LED light flickers on his face. I secretly wish I didn't have to hear the repetitive sounds of their simple chorus and constant beeping.

He has my attention. *"Where did he get this from,"* I ask myself. I wait for more.

He raises his eyebrows and shoots a quick glance my way, seeing my impatient expression. Afraid I will order him to turn off the tablet, he quickly continues.

"They are killing everyone, smashing villages, making tidal waves and then an asteroid crashes into the earth," my son elaborates.

Stunned at his apocalyptic description of the end of our civilization, I wonder if he is talking from a game point-of-view or if he has really considered the fragility of the world he is graduating into.

But he is only ten years old!

He's got my attention and he sees that he does. He fears that he has mistakenly demonstrated his need for time away from the internet delivery of apps for games, TV shows with superhero battles, and movies that constantly exhibit the power of evil, intending to entice the weak and immature mind.

"Then God fights back," my son continues. "He resurrects everyone and defeats Satan. Jesus comes with the angels and a mighty sword that slashes Satan down. The devil is sent back into hell and kept there in a cage, in a fiery bit of hell."

He turns his attention back to the video game, expecting that he has given me enough to satisfy my inquiry and squelch my opposition to his excessive gaming time.

Wow!

I am amazed. My son has just paraphrased the Book of Revelation in the Bible as it predicts the apocalyptic end of the world.

I hope he never sees it happen. My urgent wish is that he does not have to live through "hell's revenge." But seriously, I wonder how close the end of our time is.

I then think about the struggles of the present. Is hell having its revenge on us now? Haven't I lived there, on the spiritual battlefield, with the war yet unresolved?

What are the "monsters" Satan will send? I ponder for insight into spiritual things, that which is known in our mind from our soul, that which ultimately drives and defines our lives.

Perhaps the monsters are here, already. The battle for my life, and that of my son, is raging, and now it comes closer to a child previously sheltered in innocence.

"I have to fight for my son," I caution and urge myself.

And this is where our story begins.

In each stage of life we encounter the fury of hell, hell's revenge for God's love. Life is a journey marked by the intervention of the spiritual entities, good and evil.

Satan always attacks when we are weak and vulnerable. Perceiving the battle reveals the enemy, and we must have the victory; we must conquer the monsters that come into our lives at each stage: a young boy losing his innocence to such things, and his father, a mature man determined to teach and protect his son, and hoping in the end to have done well.

But in order to guide my son through the battlefield of life, I have to first learn from my struggles, some won, some lost. This story will be based on the understanding I have gleaned from my past, the wisdom of my experience, but the characters and what happens to them is fictional.

Oh yes, there is one more thing before our story begins. You will notice that I have changed my son's title. You are wondering why.

We all suffer in a vacuum of un-fulfillment. We desire something more, even meaning for our lives. This is the basis of the enticement, the lure to evil's power. Our lives represent our quest for purpose and many are attracted to the acclaim of its prestige.

But only God is power supreme. Satan wants His throne and sovereignty – hence the devil's insatiable desire for revenge. And the conflict continues.

But Satan's war, his hatred, his torture and killing, is not to be elevated by this author, as it is magnified by other writers as being something to be desired, even admired - worshipped!

God's position is one of repose, despite the attacks targeted against Him and his followers. Our Heavenly Father is unshaken, unmoved, and unconcerned with Satan's revenge. God is unchangeable and immoveable. The presence of His Grace is omnipotent, omnipresent, and omniscient.

Only God will bring repose, such stability and peace into your life, as the battle rages all around you. This is the story worth telling, the only lesson worth learning. And ultimately, the decisions you make will define your destiny.

When a life event impacts with great loss and the potential for change we must strive to understand "hell's revenge and heaven's repose". Look for such interpretation at the end of eventful chapters.

What happens in the end has already been recorded. A rider called "Faithful and True," comes on a white horse. He has a sharp sword. His name is, "King of Kings and Lord of Lords." Satan's generals are captured and imprisoned and his armies are destroyed. Then, Satan is bound in the Abyss for 1,000 years. (Rev. 19:11-21 and 20:1-3)

No one knows when the end will come. The details of the events that unfold during the end times are unknown, and the following account is fictional. As I have studied the Book of Revelation, I am impressed with the need for perseverance. There is advice and there are warnings for those who will live and endure the coming travail.

With the opening of the sixth seal, there is a great earthquake.

Today the United States Geological Survey says there is a 72% probability that a similar quake will occur within thirty years.

Are we living in the eleventh hour?

Prelude

What does history teach us?

1863:

"Papa, Papa! What is that noise?" A boy listens intently to hear a faint boom, boom, boom!

It was the evening of a hot and humid June day, late in the month. The Daniels lived on a small farm, about 30 acres, on the roadway that leads to Greencastle, Pennsylvania.

"They are the drums of war," Levi reluctantly tells his four year old son Amos. The boy is holding a toy soldier roughly carved out of a piece of hemlock that had been discarded near the wood pile. This wooden soldier wears a jacket colored in blue.

"But why? Why are they coming here?"

Papa is deep in thought as he gazes toward the roadway that disappears into the southern horizon. How should he prepare for these unwanted visitors? Is his family in danger?

He remembers the words of a Negro spiritual he heard months earlier while traveling north to Chambersburg. The tune is one he had since often whistled while doing morning chores. He went to the city for tools and supplies, and to see a lawyer, determined to put his house in order, as he worried about the threat of an invasion by the Confederate Army.

"Say, brothers, will you meet us on Canaan's happy shore."

"Glory, glory, hallelujah. Glory, glory, hallelujah. Glory, glory, hallelujah, for ever, evermore!" (chorus)

"By the grace of God we'll meet you, where parting is no more."

(repeat chorus)

"Jesus lives and reigns forever, on Canaan's happy shore."

"Glory, glory, hallelujah. Glory, glory, hallelujah. Glory, glory, hallelujah, for ever, evermore!"

(Say, Brothers)

It was a time when faith flourished, even as the loss of humanity was inconceivable. The personal losses suffered by survivors were incomprehensible. Tragedy invaded the course of their lives with change that was permanent. Unwillingly embroiled in the conflict, husbands embraced their wives and parents sheltered their children, looking beyond, grasping onto hope anchored in their religious beliefs. These were the foundations of Christianity taught by the parson in the little white church with the tall pointed steeple covered in tin and adorned with a wooden cross on top, painted silver. It is surrounded by a white picket fence that also encloses the cemetery at its side but provides little protection from critter intruders. Groundhogs are a menace here.

Confederate troops came upon the Daniels farm as they marched toward Gettysburg. Looters trailed behind with wagons for their booty. They burned the Daniels' barns, corn cribs, and animal pens after taking the cows, goats, pigs, and chickens suitable for food, and killing less desirables, vermin in their eyes. Papa Levi was spotted running from his hiding place behind a coup and was shot in the calf of his left leg, then left for dead. His tibia was shattered. Days later, his lower leg was removed, cut off just above the knee.

As the week unfolded at nearby Gettysburg there were 50,000 causalities. It was the turning point of the great Civil War that killed more than 620,000 soldiers.

Surviving Union troops reformed and marched from the farms of southern Pennsylvania in pursuit of the retreating Confederate Army. But the words of their stirring anthem had changed.

"John Brown's body lies a-mouldering in the grave. His soul's marching on!"

"Glory, glory, hallelujah. Glory, glory, hallelujah. Glory, glory, hallelujah, his soul's marching on! He's gone to be a soldier in the army of the Lord! His soul's marching on! (chorus)

"John Brown's knapsack is strapped upon his back! His soul's marching on!"

(repeat chorus)

"His pet lambs will meet him on the way; They go marching on!"

(repeat chorus)

"They will hang Jeff Davis to a sour apple tree! As they march along!

"Now, three rousing cheers for the Union; now, three rousing cheers for the Union; now three rousing cheers for the Union; As we are marching on!"

(John Brown's Body)

In the next year the Daniels family made the strenuous trek to the West, hoping to find a new and prosperous nation. It was 1864. They longed for peace and stability even as the war raged on.

But there, in the thriving town that became their new home, they would soon meet another disaster, even as the enduring turmoil of war continued to ravage the lives of those striving to recover back east. The drum's rhythmic boom had ceased; the canon's blasting had finally been silenced, but the suffering in great loss continued.

Then the great man who guided the nation divided, died in row house, a cheap boarding house, the Petersen House, with an assassin's bullet in his head. At 7:22 am on April 15, 1865, Abraham Lincoln, the 16th president of the United States, went to the great beyond.

The nation's mourning resurged. It was nearly 24 hours before the news reached San Francisco, California, and a man appearing to be much older than his years, cried softly despite his attempt to hold back the tears.

"Papa! Papa, why are you crying?"

He stood feebly on his wooden peg leg, and leaned against his wife as they sang in church later that week.

And once again the words that accompanied the familiar refrain had changed. The new hymn was introduced as **"The Battle Hymn of the Republic."**

And the earth shook violently.

It was 7:53 am that clear October morning of 1868. Levi Daniels had secured a job as the cobbler's assistant, working at his bench long hours in the modest shop located on his block. He was preparing to leave for his employment when their upstairs living quarters began shaking.

A tall and solidly constructed hutch banged against the horse hair plaster wall. It had been heavy and sturdy enough to survive the wagon's long haul. Its doors fell open and a ruby colored dish tumbled toward the floor. Then the cabinet toppled over, falling onto the bassinet.

"Mama! Mama, where are you?"

Deidra and Darren's great-great-grandfather was only a small child when he asked these haunting questions during events that were ultimate in influencing their destiny.

The Hayward earthquake was violent; it measured 7 on the Richter scale, and claimed the lives of 30 unsuspecting residents of the Bay Area.

One of the victims was a newborn baby.

Levi Daniels succumbed later that year to pneumonia, but not before he passed the secret on to his son. He told Amos about the small wooden box, one hidden in their home, the box that he brought from Pennsylvania.

Three Generations Later:

1968:

"Fred, the TV's not working."

He peered over the top of his newspaper, the Detroit Free Press, and gave his wife a look of contempt.

"C'mon Fred! The storm last night probably blew the antenna off. Ethel wants to watch her cartoon. She's whining and it's about to drive me crazy." Mrs. Barbara Daniels was slightly more demanding than usual during her second pregnancy. She was often tired. A steam kettle in the kitchen began to whistle softly, even as she began to boil inside with impatience. She returned his glare.

"Huckleberry Hound is starting soon!" she demanded.

Fred, a mason and carpenter who was self-employed, should have been working that Wednesday, June 5, 1968, but the heavy rain that fell the night before filled his trench with water. The form he constructed for the footer was soaked and twisted by the dirt that fell against it. He couldn't pour concrete in the mud. He inspected the construction site a 7 a.m., and then returned home, planning to fetch supplies after a late breakfast. It was now 9 am and he still hadn't eaten.

Much of the work to prepare for the building's foundation would now have to be redone. Fred was simmering with disgust and hot to the touch, much like the bottom of that kettle as it sat on the natural gas flame. This job was already looking like a series of problems that would produce little profit for this contractor.

"Put the kid in her room," he ordered grimly with a frown. He wondered why it was taking so long for his meal to be ready. He was losing precious time.

The young mother placed both hands firmly on her hips and stomped her right foot against the floor, causing her apron to flare as she shouted one word, "Fred!" These were the signs of an imminent attack about to be launched. Her eyes grew wide.

But before she hollered back at him, Fred jumped up and darted across the room, tossing his paper to the floor. The sports page drifted toward the bay window. It was occupied by a side table that provided a prominent place for the telephone, one of two in the house. It was black plastic with a large rotary dial on a sloped front, designed by Western Electric. The coiled cord that kept the receiver leashed to the rectangular base was knotted into a ball.

As he threw it open, the rear door banged against the side of the refrigerator reaffirming the small dent there and then the screen's frame slapped at its jambs. He kicked at a tree limb that lay across the uneven flagstone walkway. It led to an old outhouse at the rear of their narrow lot, now used as a yard shed.

The Daniels family had relocated to Detroit from San Francisco in 1955. Fred's father hoped for a place on the auto assembly line, after he lost his job with a ship builder that downsized. Calvin Daniels was already looking forward to his retirement in just four years. Detroit was mass producing millions of cars. He took a job with American Motors, sealing windshields in Rambler station wagons. His employer was a new startup in a former Ford plant that consolidated its operations the year before. Gone was Nash, and Hudson, the proud manufacturer of the sedan Calvin drove to work on days when the electric trolley wasn't running. He opened a checking account at the National Bank of Detroit, and rented a safety deposit box there for family valuables. His wife complained about the annual fee, but Calvin was unrelenting and determined to keep it.

"The whole house swayed back and forth," he bellowed in a baritone voice. With his grandkids on each knee, he would sway them from side to side, grasping their upper arms tightly. Timothy was 3 years old and his cousin Ethel was 2. He'd then pull them together and toss them into the air as he proclaimed in melody, "and the walls came tumbling down." They knew the playful skit, having enjoyed it many times before. Timothy was the son of Fred's sister, Millie.

"More Papa, More!"

Grandpa gently sat them onto the floor from where they immediately sprang up and began to run across the room toward Granny who suddenly appeared with the cookie jar.

"I'll never forget it," he continued, looking toward his son. "It was like we were on a skiff, in rough seas."

"Fred, I can still feel the burn," he whined as his throat grew dry and raspy. It was the great San Francisco earthquake and fire of 1906 that he remembered with lingering anxiety. "I was only twelve years old, but I'll never forget it. Everything was falling onto the floor. My father was yelling for us to get out of the house, pointing to the rear." His eyes filled with water and he coughed lightly. "We had a small back yard where nothing would collapse and fall onto us," he explained. "Amos, my father, your grandfather, ran back into the house after mother. In the moonlight I saw the rear wall fall into the center. They barely made it out of the front door. "

"It was still dark, ya know. Early morning. I almost fell out of my bunk."

"Your grandmother came running toward us shouting something. I think she was tellin' us to get on the ground. I had already lost my balance and fallen down. She came and huddled us together, like a hen pulls in her chicks. We sat there on the ground in the dark and waited. It seemed like forever. I could hear hollerin' and crying. Soon there was an eerie light shinin' from down the street."

"My brother asked about father. He had gone to check on a neighbor. Then we began to smell the smoke. The light got brighter."

"The fire spread quickly. Eighty percent of the city was destroyed, you know."

"Our house burned up, and we lost everything, but we were lucky to get out alive. The only thing he saved was that box, the one he got from his father. " He paused and wiped at his eyes as he cleared his throat. "Levi was my grandfather," he explained. "Most of the city burned that day," Calvin continued. "You know, more than three thousand people died.... some of them my school buddies."

"Jacob, my younger brother said we gotta git outta there. Mother formed us into a chain, olders with youngsters bein' the in-betweens. We were real scared, and held hands real tight. We climbed over some boards that were alongside the house, I mean the rubble, and went out into the middle of the cobblestone street. We ran against the wind, away from the fire. But it was bad. I could feel the heat and the smoke is still burnin' in my throat."

From a vantage point about thirty feet away from the wood sided house, Fred could clearly see the roof. It was covered with asphalt shingles that curled at the edges, on a moderate pitch. The roof was already dry from the morning sun.

The TV antenna had toppled over, now tilted toward the ridge and resting upon it. It was a pole anchored by a tripod of short legs screwed through the shingles and attached firmly to the roof boards. Projected four feet into the air, the main tube was mounted on a swivel bracket and extended out in both directions from the center post, parallel to the ground. It had intersecting perpendicular tubes that appeared like fingers that were supposed to rake the air waves for its faint signal. It looked like a miniature electrical grid. Energy and information now came from somewhere unknown, and it was all invisible. One had to first catch it, and then it would travel through a wire. This homeowner reluctantly and suspiciously accepted these modern conveniences demanded by his wife. Everything was changing. Rapidly!

Fred turned to see the wooden ladder lying in the weeds under the hedges that marked the property line. It was wet and slippery. He would have to first climb up onto the rear porch roof and then hoist himself over the dormer wall and onto the main roof. He had done this many times before, grasping the bottom of the facia board that overhung the front of the soffit. He squeezed its edge with the fingertips of his left hand, stepped on the window sill, and throwing his right leg upward with a slight jump he intended to latch onto the skyhook, which of course wasn't there. It was a balancing act, a calculated risk dependent on stamina, and it looked like the feat of a circus acrobat. With bad luck plaguing him today, he considered pulling up the ladder and using it a second time to reach the top of the house, even though it would likely puncture holes in the porch roof.

He paused as he raised the ladder to its vertical position and exhaled through open lips with a long and exasperating sigh, hoping this would not be the day he would fall.

Coming through the kitchen he could hear the television set crackling. It was a large glass tube in a console with a record player in one end and a radio in the other. The black-and-white picture was flickering as bars scrolled quickly, rolling from bottom to top, in continuous, mesmerizing motion. Barbara was already turning the large tuner knob. It was stiff and clicked with each segment of the rotation.

"There! That's better."

She made another rapid click.

"No, go back one."

She stood alongside her husband and then stooped down to pick up Ethel who was tugging at her long skirt. She was nearing the end of her term, and strained to lift the thirty-six pound child above her womb.

The TV's long rectangular box was perched on tapered legs, about seven inches above the hardwood floor. It had a woven fabric, tanish-mauve in color, covering large round speakers which were fourteen inches in diameter and mounted on the front at each end of the appliance; the picture simmered from a glass window in the center. The radio had stopped working shortly after the Daniels purchased the used entertainment center from a customer whose house he remodeled.

Airing was a special newscast. A reporter was saying something about Kennedy.

"Did you hear that?" Fred demanded. "Oh my gawd… not again!" He still had raw emotions as he remembered the assassination of President John Fitzgerald Kennedy, not quite five years earlier.

"Hush! I can't hear," Barbara responded. "Oh no, you're right. He's been shot and they've taken him to the hospital."

That night Mrs. Daniels went into labor. Fred rushed his wife to the hospital, and with his little girl sleeping in his arms, paced across the waiting room, back and forth. It was just after 4 am, Thursday, June 6, 1968, that Joseph arrived with promise for their future. Fred kissed his wife on the forehead and congratulated her on her successful delivery. In his mind she was a strong woman, and a good mother. Now he was again a proud father. He had a son.

But the Daniels' joy was dampened by the news that was passed from person to person, whispered in the hallways of the hospital, ear to ear. Even Grandpa Calvin seemed more interested in current events when he limped into the room on his cane, visiting the hospital two days later. Senator Robert Francis Kennedy had died that very morning, just before their son was born.

It was one hundred years, short of 19 weeks and four days, from the anniversary of the Hayward Earthquake that had claimed the young life of this newborn's great-great-great-great Aunt Martha, also an infant.

No one was remembering that tragedy, or talking about it, even as history loomed over them with a warning for their future.

SECTION ONE

OUR DECLINE – we are conflicted. In spiritual

rebellion opposites become combative.

In the time before the great quake, Americans lived in lavish pursuit of *pleasure* and self gratification. Lost was concern for their fellow man.

The rich increased in the opulence of their wealth and then became *passive* in possession of their great *sufficiency*.

The poor, *angry* in their plight, increased in *discontent*.

Society was obviously headed for *rebellion*, the classes eager to clash, their cause of entitlement inflamed by the propositions of *false religion*, unto a civil conflict greater than any other known in the land.

America had lost the unity of the faith of her founding fathers. There was no basis for reconciliation among the peoples.

But in looking back, one must now perceive the greater spiritual forces at work in our country and the world.

Chapter 1

"They have builded Him an altar in the evening dews and damps,"

Anger unresolved produces the cynicism of lasting discontent.

Conscious awareness can be extremely painful at the time of a tragic separation.

1994:

Fred Daniels died on July 8, young in leaving this world at the age of sixty. He had suffered internal injuries after falling more than thirty feet from a third-story roof on a row house. It was a chilly April morning the day of his accident and the slate shingles were covered in thin, black ice, a frost unannounced by the weatherman.

His son Joseph had married young, more by requirement than by choice. His romp in the back seat of his 1975 Chevy Caprice Classic resulted in an unexpected commitment that suddenly forced him at the age of 18 to appear at the altar of matrimony. He finished high school, married that June, and quickly joined the Marines.

In April of that same year, 1986, President Ronald Reagan had ordered the U.S. air and naval forces to conduct bombing raids on terrorist installations in Libya. The military operation was successful and a spirit of patriotism soared in the United States. But Joseph was still angry about the bombing of the barracks occupied by American soldiers in Beirut three years earlier. It had left an indelible impression on him. **Those paying the ultimate price in their quest for world peace numbered 241, and most of the causalities were U.S. Marines. Many were sleeping at the time of the attack.**

Joseph's young bride, Terry, also a high school student, gave birth to the twins on October 20. He was somewhere overseas by then. The children never met their father who broke off contact and simply disappeared. Terry continually pressed her father-in-law for contact information. He denied knowing of his son's whereabouts and stepped in with financial assistance to help fill the void.

"Mommy, do I have to go?" Deidra, a strapping eight-year-old, asked her mother.

"Yeah, it will be boring," her twin brother Darren quickly echoed to reinforce his sister's complaint.

Relatives often referred to them as the "Double D's," or the "dynamic duo." As partners in crime, drawing support and strength from one another, the twins had certainly found enough mischief as young children. It was a difficult time for their single mother of three. Terry was feeling much older than her age, as she was hardly more than a child herself.

"Now you know how much your grandfather loved you, and…" she paused in reflection. "He was always there for us, whenever we needed him."

Tears glistened in the corners of the young woman's eyes. "He was a good man," she declared firmly. "I hated to see him suffer so much after his fall."

"Deidra," she continued. "Check and see what your little sister is doing."

Cynthia came five years after the twins. Her father was unknown to them. Terry's second and final attempt at a meaningful relationship had also failed.

The three-year-old would be dropped off at Aunt Ethel's, where a sitter from her church volunteered to assist the family during their time of bereavement.

Sitting on a folding chair with a plush padded seat, Darren felt safe and secure between his mother and twin sister. Deidra was always the bold one. She garnered the most attention from relatives at events such as this, and Darren welcomed the diversion. The funeral speaker, a pastor from a church his grandfather attended a few years ago, was a stranger to the boy. His mind drifted, and he remembered the last meaningful conversation he had with his grandfather. At the time he was surprised by its serious tone, and the intensity expressed by "Grandpa."

Fred had been hospitalized for several days after hernia surgery. Terry took the kids in for a visit, hoping to cheer him up. After several minutes of small talk, he asked to speak privately to Darren who flushed with embarrassment and fear as the others reluctantly left the room.

He remembered hearing his pulse pounding in his right ear, like the bass drum of the band as it paraded by.

"Darren, come here." Fred looked to the boy's concern. "It's okay. There's something I want to tell you."

The boy pressed against the hospital bed after bumping the IV stand. "It's okay." His grandpa smiled and reached for his hand.

"We Daniels have a secret treasure," he said plainly, determined to catch the boy's full attention. "It is the man's job to keep it safe."

"A treasure?" Darren fumbled softly. His eyes got big as they connected with his grandfather's. "You mean, like a pirate's?" he suggested.

"No. Well, not like that. It came to me from my father, but it all started with my Great-Grandfather Levi." He looked at his grandson for understanding.

"Grandpa, what's in the treasure?" Darren demanded with new enthusiasm.

"Well, I'm not exactly sure. Like I said, it's a secret."

"Can I see it?"

"No… and you must keep this a secret. It's our secret, yours and mine."

Darren displayed a look of disappointment and confusion.

"Promise me that you will keep our secret," his grandfather demanded.

The boy nodded his head in affirmation.

"I keep it in the bank," Fred whispered. "Someday, you will be in charge of keeping it safe. When the time comes, you will remember that I told you about it. You will remember our secret then."

"When will that be," Darren asked, disappointed with the details of this revelation.

"When you get older," he answered. "Do you understand?"

"I guess so…"

"Good boy!" Fred smiled and squeezed Darren's hand. "Give your grandpa a kiss, and then go get the others."

Darren willingly complied and turned to leave the room.

"Remember, you must keep our secret."

The boy paused and looked back at his grandfather. Darren was frowning with the unwelcome responsibility.

"Okay, I'll try."

From his seat in the third row during the funeral service, Darren could see his grandfather's forehead and nose protruding above the rim of the casket. Grandpa looked like he was napping, with eyes closed, but different, and somehow, Darren felt disconnected by the unfamiliarity of the corpse that lay before him.

Despite the fact that he had not attended church services in recent years, Fred was still regarded as a religious man. Tears streamed down her cheeks as Terry was consumed with her memory of the deceased. She trembled slightly, feeling loss and fear, trying to hide her sobs.

It was the third week of January of that year. She and the children were sitting with Fred and Barbara in their dining room for a family dinner. Fred said grace, and prayed for God to preserve His truth, asking for patience for the shortcomings of mankind. Terry remembered being impressed with the oddity of his reverent request.

After eating, the kids were sent into the living room to watch TV. Barbara jumped up and began clearing dishes from the table. Terry found herself alone, sitting near her father-in-law, still solemn.

"Did you hear about the earthquake last week?" he asked.

"Not much," she answered with curiosity at the question. "It was in California, wasn't it?"

"That's right," he said, "They always get my attention." He paused and scraped his knife on the edge of his dinner plate, anticipating the cleanup. "My father used to tell the story about his experience with one in San Francisco." He looked at his son's wife and felt an absence ripping at his heart. He should have been sharing this moment with him, but Joseph was rarely spoken of these days.

The Northridge earthquake occurred on January 17, with its epicenter in Reseda, a community in the San Fernando Valley region of Los Angeles. It lasted only slightly more than 10 seconds, but with a magnitude of 6.7 it caused considerable damage and resulted in 57 deaths.

It seemed that these days the public had become all too familiar with the earth's rumblings and gave them little concern.

Terry looked down at her plate. A few peas lingered along the silver line that encircled it. She felt that it was lady-like to leave some of her food there. She seldom asked for seconds, and almost never did so in the presence of her in-laws.

Then the silence between them became uncomfortable as she still wondered about the meaning of his words, and the purpose of this family dinner.

"Are you concerned?" she blurted, and then surprised at her words, feared that she had pried too deeply. "I mean, do you think it will happen here." She glanced up.

He was still looking at the remnants of his meal. She also dropped her head.

"No, it's not that, exactly," he answered in a serious tone. "But it is a sign."

Terry felt the impulse to fire out another quick question, but bit her lower lip instead.

"Sometimes I wonder," he sighed. "About the prophecy of the end of time," he continued.

Fred looked directly at Terry and their eyes met. His gaze was distant and steely.

"When the church stops proclaiming the truth," he paused for affect, "then I'm afraid, my dear, that the end is near."

Terry swallowed hard, a little annoyed for not wanting to be confronted by such pessimism.

"But what is '*the truth*'?" she felt a surge of resentment, like acid in the larynx. "There are so many religions and denominations."

Fred felt the tension also. He appeared to be concentrating as he balanced his dinner knife on top of the high arch of the fork's handle. Silence permeated the room except for the sound of silly tunes penetrating the wall from the adjoining room. Barbara was already washing dishes in the kitchen.

"You must lose your life to find it."

The plate clanged as he dropped his silverware upon it. He cleared his throat loudly. "The Holy Spirit will show you the way."

The silence of the viewing room brought her back to Fred's funeral. There was shuffling in the aisles, and the pallbearers reluctantly came forward. It was time to say her final goodbye. Terry truly dreaded this moment.

Like the gloom of a sunless November day, the loss felt by Fred's sudden demise lingered long into the next month, even as the days began to grow shorter. It was the third Saturday in August when Terry remained in bed one morning, thinking about her life, and feeling sad about the lackluster summer her kids were experiencing. With a hot muggy day in the forecast, in the spur of that hopeful moment, she decided to take them to Lake George State Park, hoping they would carelessly frolic on the beach and splash in the cool, spring-fed waters. This day, she reasoned, was good for an old-fashioned picnic. She hoped for revival.

At the lake, near the changing rooms, Terry met a former high school classmate who was endowed with pride and committed to endless chatter, surprised at their unexpected reunion and happy for the opportunity to compare achievements, full of updates and bragging about her picture-perfect life. Terry was looking for an escape.

Then a mother holds the limp body, the shell of her child, alive and laughing only thirty minutes earlier. She saw her running into the lake's chilly water, bouncing on its sandy bottom, and splashing in laughter. But in this dreadful moment, this mother struggles with the comprehension of reality. She is conscious, and aware of her daughter's demise, but her mind resists the cruel fact of the horrific loss.

Terry caught a glimpse of Deidra splashing Darren in his face. "Where is Cindy?" she yelled in their direction. "Excuse me," she pushed past her captor. "I don't see my daughter."

"Cindy... Cindy, where are you?" Panic rises. She nearly tumbled forward as her feet urgently splashed in the water, reaching for the bottom that had fallen away. "Deidra! Where is Cindy?"

She received only a blank look in reply.

A frequent visitor of the park approached Terry. "Are you OK?" he asked, already knowing that the woman was panicked.

"It's my daughter!" she growled. "I can't find my three-year-old daughter!"

He turned away from her and began addressing the crowd that suddenly formed there. Silence permeated the atmosphere. Shouting, laughing, teasing - they were heard no more.

"I want everyone to form a line at the water's edge," he instructed firmly. "Now stand about two feet apart, hold hands, and walk into the water."

"No, no! It cannot be!" Terry was shouting as she ran toward the beach house. "She must have gone in there."

She was almost at the door when she heard a stranger proclaim the doom she dreaded most. "Here she is! I got her!"

The separation is more than she can bear, and her emotions flood upon her like the raging torrent of a broken dam. She is suddenly submerged, and her pain is smothered as she tries to understand, looking as one on the ocean's bottom to the light dancing upon the surface. The life beyond, it is blurry, and she dimly sees what was her happy life, just moments before, as she is about to expel her final breath and allow the salt water to painfully fill and press upon the inside of her lungs.

Her life was complete. Now it is full with incomprehensible fear.

Who is that still speaking at her, now welling with tears and reaching for an embrace? The distraction fades in her consciousness, and anger begins to tell her that this is what caused her to lose the most precious thing in her life, her young daughter. She was only three years old. Her head begins to spin. Her heart explodes.

Deidra was a young girl and a confused observer of that dreadful day, the picnic at the state park that profoundly affected and changed her life, permanently dimming the light of joy in her home. Her brother stood silently alongside as together they began to perceive the tragedy of losing their little sister. And it was worse for Deidra, as she felt responsible, having been the designated babysitter.

Hell's Revenge: these demons, lieutenants in rank, are gloating at their apparent success in hurting a young person as they intend to claim dominion in her soul. Anger and discontent intend to make a permanent residence in Deidra's life. This is a stronghold upon which they can establish the way of doubt unto denial.

Heaven's Repose: consumed in compassion, Jesus feels Terry's pain and cries for her. He understands the great loss of humanity caused by their sudden and unexpected separation. He offers an embrace of assurance and comfort that can be known nowhere else.

He promises to always be near to Deidra and her hurting heart, offering hope unknown in the earthly realm.

Cindy is carried by an angel to heaven's gate. The child has not been taken, but received, and the Savior hopes for the eventual reunion of mother and child.

Chapter 2

"I can read His righteous sentence by the dim and flaring lamps,"

With a heart that denies true love, the will is directed for fulfillment in pleasure.

Our lives are the gardens we plant: for whatsoever man sows that shall he also reap.

2000:

Darren can't find sleep in his dormitory room. After holding his eyes closed for nearly two hours, while seeking solace from thoughts deep within, another boy in the room sneezes and his eyes are jarred open again.

Deidra is located nearby in the girls' dorm of Camp Manitobaqua.

It is now the summer of 2000, and the world is still functioning, apparently having corrected the huge computers expected to crash at the beginning of the year. The conspiracy theory was called "Y2K". If the electrical grid and wireless communications were to fail, urban rioting was the expected result.

He was thinking about his sister. His twin was up to something naughty, he could sense and feel her excitement. Pleasure was calling both of their names.

They are now 14 years old, and as nature goes, puberty has possessed her with an uncanny interest in the opposite sex. Sure, Darren is also looking, but he has no desire to indulge such a curiosity.

He threw off the top of his sleeping bag, pulled his knees to his chest, and struggled to free his feet from the bag's confinement, above the place where the zipper enclosed it. He wanted to avoid its mechanical noise.

His feet quickly found their flip-flops, meticulously placed alongside his bottom bunk, and he stood, but then paused to look around the room at his dorm mates. Most were turned facing the wall. No one seemed to have noticed his intention of an imminent escape.

He could hear the crickets chirping outside, just beyond the boarded walls. The screen door was the next culprit he faced, purposed to sound an alarm with its eerie screeching sound broadcasted from its rusty hinges. Darren paused there and determined that he was justified in taking a potty break. This would be his excuse if he was caught outside. He pushed on the door's frame hard and fast and its responsive whine was minimal.

The untimely death and loss of his little sister, Cynthia, had been a prison sentence to his family. His mother had cried uncontrollably for months. The door to their apartment revolved with visits from pastors, well meaning friends, and then psychiatric counselors. Eventually, his mother, Terry, found a confidant upon which she leaned heavily. The trio began attending church, their mother sitting next to her new friend, Jessica, with the others filling the pew to its end.

It is now six years since the tragedy, and like the scars of war documented by history, the loss to this small family will never be forgotten, felt in some way, each and every day that pursues them. For Terry, it is an endless prosecution of her self-imposed sentence of criminal negligence. In her heart and mind she finds no solace in the designation of accident, but remains convicted as a felon. Her time is spent imprisoned by guilt. Drudgery.

Darren found the beginnings of resolve as he took to heart the reconciliation of religion found within the sanctuary of the healing. Deidra rejected it as simple bunk and leaned upon her determination for personal strength. She did not oppose dependency on an external force, or god, as it was now exercised in church by her mother and brother, but when she was prompted for action, her strength came from within: a determined and strong will.

Jessica's son Anthony had caught her eye. Upon entering the church and walking the aisle, she would quickly survey their destination and then posture for the position that would allow her to sit next to him. One week they secretly held hands during the benediction prayer.

Tony was a high school senior, four years her elder. Like the effect on younger children, the age difference was significant as it determined their levels of maturity and related activity. Tony was looking to score for his first time, boiling over with the masculine desire of conquest. He wanted to experience life fully. He invited Deidra to youth meetings and then urged her to attend summer camp. Darren was the third wheel, an increasingly apparent obstacle to Tony's plan. Tony and Deidra were two connected to a third, her other half, her omniscient twin brother, and this unbreakable union of siblings revealed itself in this affair much like the malcontented one of a love triangle.

Deidra was intrigued by the attention she received from a desirable male. The absence of her father had created a void and a hunger for affection even greater than that experienced by other girls her age. She wanted to be romanced and feel wanted and beautiful. She looked for a place of retreat from the disdain of her home. Her emotions and hormones were agitated like a bottle of soda pop that was briskly shaken. If the lid was released, the vent would nearly explode from the pressure within. She was feeling more alive as she distanced herself from the tragedy her family had become.

Other girls her age had restraint, safety valves tightly closed, and stability found in fulfilling relationships of family, friends, and faith. Although Terry seemed to be completely clueless of her daughter's vulnerability, Darren was well aware of her temptation. He wondered if he should ask for help, but could not bring a breach upon the trust they placed in each other. There had been many times that one covered for the other to avoid punishment, often without prior acknowledgement of the need for a cover-up. They simply knew, each for the other.

Darren held the door until it was gently replaced in full closure. It was a warm night, and a full moon lit the ground in welcome romance. But his mood was one of brooding concern.

He walked toward the lake and out upon the dock. Looking into the water, it was thick and blackish. Visibility was unrelenting, and the force of the unknown concealed under its hard surface beckoned him with the power of evil. He shook shivers off his spine.

He gazed out upon deeper water. It too called to him, but the moon was reflecting there and his countenance rallied in response to its illumination. Turning back toward the shoreline, he was suddenly startled as he saw movement within the shadows of the trees. They stood there unmoved, like pillars for life, even as the security exhibited by their presence was unraveled by unpredictable circumstances.

It was now almost 2 am. A soft breeze caught upon his face with the chill of the coming dawn.

The shadows of night are the bridges of malevolence. The person who hides there darts about, intending to conceal the acts condemned by their conscience when exposed to the light.

Darren stiffened his body and squinted for clarity. There, something moved again. Then he saw it, a distinctive form with familiarity. It was the shape of his sister.

Deidra was hiding from the moonlight, about to smash the glass which was the window of her moral compass. Darren stepped forward as a flashlight of virtue, hoping to reveal the noose his sister was about to engage.

"Deidra. Is that you?" he shouted in a harsh whisper. She suddenly froze between the trees.

"Deidra, I see you. Where are you going?"

"Oh, hi Darren," she stuttered like one caught in vandalism. "But what are you doing out here?" she queried.

"Well, I couldn't sleep. I was kind of worried about you."

She came forward and gave her twin brother a hug. "Yeah, I miss you too. But really, you're fine."

He looked into her eyes and quickly saw the deceit upon her countenance.

"Deidra! Don't do it! You will regret it. I'm warning you!"

"Darren! Relax! I'm not going to *doooo* anything."

"Deidra, I know better. It's me. Remember me, your other half, all knowing about you…"

She dropped her head and sighed. "OK, you got me."

They looked upon each other, each peering deep inside the others mind.

"I know what I'm doing," Deidra pleaded. "Please, Darren, this has to be our secret."

She hit that place of intimacy between them, the place sacred to twins.

He dropped his head as she took hold of his left hand.

"Darren, this is my life." She gently shook his hand to emphasize her statement. "I have to live it my way." She paused. "We have to start living again."

He made no verbal response but pleaded with more than his eyes. It may have been telepathy, and she clearly felt his loving concern.

She simply said, "It's OK," and then dropping his hand she turned away, and darted once again for the shadows.

Darren watched his sister continue to dodge the beams of moonlight as she made her way toward the dining hall. Several buildings in that vicinity provided the ideal place for a rendezvous with her boyfriend.

And just then he felt something new regarding her. It was more than a pause; it was more like a break, or a crack in the intense bond that firmly held them together. It was a breach of trust.

Hell's Revenge: the henchmen in Satan's command observe and report the progress they have made in influencing Deidra to take the course they persuade. Denial and Pleasure are captains in this renegade force. They will now assume command for the plan they have for her, purposing to escort her further down the pathway of self-fulfillment.

Heaven's Repose: in intercession for Deidra, the Lord commands his angels to be persistent in watching over her. They are instructed to speak to her conscience in frequent repetition. Jesus prays for her heart, knowing full well the pain she has experienced, and longing for the opportunity to touch her in healing. The angels will reaffirm Darren, giving him an extra measure of the Savior's love, thus increasing his concern and motivation for influencing his sister for remorse unto penitence.

Chapter 3

"As ye deal with my contemners, So with you my grace shall deal;"

The conscience is appeased with a scapegoat, and religious dogma serves well.

Many will respond, but the confessions of some are insincere and false.

2001:

Time stopped ticking. In the moment a person first became aware of the 911 attacks against the United States, their mind overwhelmed, paused. So did time, or so it seemed. Each will remember that moment prolonged always, and where they were when they first heard the terrible news.

The twins were in their sophomore year of high school and that morning they were in the algebra class of Mr. Edwards. He was writing out a long numerical problem on the black boards. With his back to his students their minds were beginning to drift.

Then there was an unexpected knock at the door. The teacher first looked that way as the door opened slightly, then went to speak with the person who interrupted them.

He was ashen when he stood in front of the curious 28 pupils. Edwards was mid age, and slightly overweight. He combed with his fingers over his forehead to straighten his hair and cleared his throat. "Class, I have some news. It seems that terrorists have struck against New York City, and we are asked to be on alert for emergency measures."

Dylan, the class scholar, quickly shot up his hand. "What does that mean?" Several other hands darted upwards. "Is there going to be an early dismissal?" another boy shouted out of order.

"Now let's relax. There will be an announcement soon," he reasoned. "I don't believe we are in any danger."

By now everyone was talking at the same time.

Edwards pushed the tall cart that held the TV to the front of the room and after some fiddling with remotes, a picture came into view.

The first image of the tragedy was that of one of the twin towers with smoke billowing from it. Struck with awe, there was an immediate silence that fell over the classroom.

The September 11 attacks were a series of four coordinated terrorist attacks by the Islamic terrorist group al-Qaeda. It was a Tuesday morning. The commercial airliners loaded with unsuspecting passengers crashed between 8:46 and 10:28 am. They went into the Twin Towers in lower Manhattan and another hit the Pentagon in Washington D.C. A fourth crashed into a rural area in Pennsylvania.

The total number of deaths was 2,996. Those injured numbered more than 6,000. The attacks caused $10 billion in property and infrastructure damage and $3 trillion in total costs.

America - it hurt her pride.

Suspicion quickly fell on the terrorist organization called al-Qaeda. Their leader, Osama bin Laden at first denied any

involvement. He became a hunted man with a bounty of $25 million dollars.

Soon after the attacks on the United States, President George W. Bush visited the Islamic Center of Washington D.C. on September 17. In a nationally televised broadcast, he told Americans that the majority of Muslims are peaceful, and quoted from the Qur'an. The mosque had been visited by many important dignitaries, including other U.S. Presidents.

The United States responded to the 9/11 attacks by launching a "War on Terror." It invaded Afghanistan to combat the Taliban, a Muslim group known to harbor al-Qaeda.

Many other countries, allies of the U.S., strengthened their anti-terrorism legislation and expanded their powers of government for law enforcement and intelligence agencies, purposed at preventing another attack from Muslim extremists.

2002:

President George W. Bush approves the establishment of the Guantanamo Bay detention camp for holding captured terrorists.

Located at the Guantanamo Bay Naval Base, GTMO, in Cuba, it is where prisoners are detained indefinitely and tortured for information.

2003:

Dubbed Operation Iraqi Freedom by the United States and its allies, the invasion of Iraq lasted twenty-one days. It commenced on March 20.

Tonight he felt like a fool. Joseph Daniels was overwhelmed with despondency even as the universe spoke of intrigue and opportunity. He leaned against the back of the dirt hole he dug hours earlier, his place for sleeping in the desert under the stars. The sky was clear and the naked eye could see as far as imagined. But Daniels didn't perceive anything beyond the hard surface of the expansive Milky Way unfolded before him. The sounds of the firing of weapons had ceased. A sudden silence was lurking about. Consumed by uncertainty, rather than wonder, he didn't really notice the magnificent display of the starry host. In that regard, he could have been in a planetarium, the junior high school student bored with the field trip presentation.

Joseph pondered about his life. He had been running from it for seventeen years. He was truly alone, a ranking officer who scolded and demeaned new recruits with insults empowered by his own guilt. But why? What was the purpose of it all?

He wondered about his girlfriend and reluctant bride. Terry was young and timid, and he had forced himself upon her, burning with the passion of the moment. They were two kids, irresponsible in immature love, and it was lust unleashed that fired his engine. He wished he could relive that moment. He would be tenderer now.

She was already crying when he met her at McDonalds, sliding onto the vinyl of the booth across from her. He quickly suggested an abortion, and her sobbing increased. He remembers looking at her with pity. If a mirror could reflect back to him now, he would be ashamed. It would show uncaring and selfishness all over his face.

She was still pretty, her red hair bobbing on her thin shoulders, draped in white cotton. When she raised her head pleadingly, black streaks marred her face. Her eyes were swollen and red.

"Terry, baby, let's get out of here," he suggested and reached for her hand. Joseph was thinking of the private lane that dead ended in the woods. It was a popular parking place.

She looked down at the tears splattered on the table. "Joey, we have to get married," she whispered and sighed. "There isn't any other way."

The wedding was in a small country church, one known to Fred, his father, from his childhood days. As he waited in a small front room cluttered with hymnals and musty old choir gowns, sweat was rolling down his cheeks. He yanked once again at his collar, and then unbuttoned it. His dad gave him that all too familiar look of disapproval. He was the groom's best man.

Terry walked down the aisle with Barbara, her impending mother-in-law. The bride's mother was deceased; a victim of breast cancer, and her father was M.I.A.

Joseph was unable to subvert a slight grin as he recalled the meeting with Pastor Jim, two weeks prior to the nuptials. What a joke! How could he have seriously agreed to marry them? Joseph was told to repent of his infidelities. Had he done so? Of course not, but what else could he have said?

Still, Terry was a desirable lover, and likely a good prospect to be a submissive wife. She would probably be a good mother, but it was an uncertainty that ate at his gut like an ulcer. What if she flew the coup?

What if she got sick, like her mother did? He'd be left holding the dirty diaper bag staring at a crying brat.

And what about the baby? There was something about this trek into the desert that had worn him down. Joseph allowed his mind to raise questions he had not permitted in prior situations that were also life threatening. He wondered if he was a father, though undeserving of the title. Did he have a son, or, perhaps a daughter?

Joseph thought about the job his father had offered in his construction company. He would be a laborer, paid seven dollars an hour. He should make enough to rent a mobile home at the nearby park, as the locals called it. His father said it was a start. It was something to build on. Joseph wondered if his dad was retired. Perhaps he was sitting under a shade tree right now, fishing pole in hand, and listening to the babbling of a brook, as it promoted peace.

Peace – there was none in this forbidden place. The sun would soon return with its scorching heat. They were a band of tortured souls. Inside they felt worse than they looked on the outside, their leathery, dark skin so dry, cracked and blotched, covering over the grim faces they wore like masks. He wondered who would die this day. Suddenly he was overwhelmed with a strong feeling, one he had not known for many years. He wanted to go home, if there was one for him still.

And what about Mom? He hoped she was healthy. She deserved a good life. He determined to write her a letter. Imagine that – a note from her long lost son, and after so many years assumed dead.

The scorched earth was already glowing in the east. A sunray, the first of the dreaded day, broke upon his face, weary in sleeplessness. A projectile whistled above his head and sand exploded in the air about twenty feet behind. The enemy had pinpointed the location of his squadron. Someone began to cough as green gas drifted toward them. Seconds mattered now as he counted them in his trained mind. He first grabbed for his gas mask. The glass before his eyes fogged and the sound of his heavy breathing banged in his brain, reeling in remorse. But there was no fear here, only a determination to follow protocol. This is when the intensive training of the Marines paid off. The drills were designed to consume and control the fearful. *Follow the instructions, do the drill.* In this moment there was nothing else.

Someone was yelling. It should have been him shouting orders. They scrambled to their feet. The wind was blowing like the sand blaster in the auto body shop. Visibility was quickly fading. Something floated in the wind. It was only paper. Pages of a torn Bible were blowing with the Iraqi sand.

A Christian nation has invaded a Muslim nation.

The U.S. sent 130,000 soldiers into the Middle East for the invasion of Iraq. The effort deposed the Ba'athist government of Saddam Hussein. The invasion was primarily a conventionally fought war as American forces captured Baghdad, the capital of Iraq. The mission was to disarm Iraq of weapons of mass destruction. Since the 9-11 attacks, there was a greater emphasis on the security of the U.S. Iraq failed to disarm itself of alleged nuclear, chemical, and biological weapons. 139 U.S. soldiers were killed and 551 wounded. Iraqi fatalities are estimated at 30,000 to their army and 7,269 civilians.

Saddam Hussein, the fifth President of Iraq, was captured on December 13, 2003. He was located during "Operation Red Dawn," a U.S. military effort in the town of ad-Dawr, near Tikrit, Iraq. He was living in squalor at a small farm and was hiding underground in a spider hole at the time of his arrest. He had been president of the country for nearly 24 years.

2004:

Osama bin Laden finally claims responsibility for the 9-11 attacks on the U.S.

Four American contractors are killed in an ambush in Fallujah, Iraq, on March 31. While working for a security company, their vehicle was hit by rocket-propelled grenades and small arms fire. Their charred and mutilated bodies were dragged through the streets. Two of the bodies were hanged from a bridge.

Five days later six people are killed and many others wounded as U.S. troops clashed with militants in Fallujah for more than two hours, bombing residential neighborhoods with rockets and cluster bombs. This action was done in an avowed retaliation for the deaths of the American contractors.

Darren stood at the edge of the swell and gazed into the horizon. He had seen the ocean only once before. When he was a child his grandparents, Fred and Barbara, took him to Ocean Grove, New Jersey, for a weekend conference they attended. The twins spent most of their time in their hotel room watching TV and throwing pillows at each other.

It was a hot day in North Carolina. He and Deidra were guests of Aunt Ethel, Uncle Charlie and their three children, Larissa, 11, Shawn, 9, and Alana, 5. The twins had just graduated from high school and the trip was offered as a graduation present. Deidra hedged on the deal, saying she could get herself to the beach if she wanted to go there. She finally agreed to join the family entourage when permission was granted for her new boyfriend, Kyle, to accompany them. He would bunk with her twin brother who was at this moment mesmerized by the motion of the overlapping waves. The fresh salty air made his nostrils swell. His hair was beginning to curl in the humidity.

Darren wanted to relax after the tedious road trip. All eight crammed with luggage and beach equipment into the Sworsens' Chrysler Town and Country. If Deidra wasn't whining, she was giggling with Kyle, as she practically sat on his lap. His hands were hidden from view. Darren kept his head turned toward the window and watched the countryside as it raced by. Trying to be polite, Aunt Ethel argued softly with her husband, Mr. Sworsen, mostly about the route he was taking and his driving, and then scolded her brood more loudly.

They finally pulled onto the gravel driveway of a raised ranch located two and one-half blocks from the beach. The van's electric door slid open, a soda can and food wrappers fell to the ground, and the passengers nearly popped out, like the air that rushes from a bag of potato chips upon its first opening. They were likewise crunched, but not broken, and everyone immediately agreed that this was a good start to their vacation. With a key in her hand, Ethel led the assault against the rental, rushing to the front door, as most everyone was anxious to explore their new digs. Deidra and Kyle lingered in the van to steal a kiss, and Darren paused near some dry grass, to take it all in, anxious to see the ocean.

It seemed to Darren that his sister was becoming distant. She teased him less often and was less confiding with the details of her varied exploits. The innocence he knew in her eyes was gone. She had pursued the call of pleasure, and somehow it had changed her. Perhaps it was simply maturity, inevitable in time.

Still, he sensed that he was losing his childhood companion, his closest and best friend in the world. This trip had showed promise for a renewal of their relationship, but then Kyle joined the troop.

The ocean represented something so much greater than his life had provided. Darren longed to understand his past and the full consequence of its tragedies, with insight for his future. He was standing on the threshold of a new life, but felt dread more than hope.

He had only been away for thirty minutes but immediately confronted guilt as he returned to their very modest vacation villa. Most of the van had already been unloaded. A few boxes of food stuff lingered behind with his lone suitcase. The others had already claimed their rooms and were likely changing into their swim suits.

"Sorry," he gestured toward Ethel. She returned a puzzled look. "I would have stayed to help."

"No problem, dear," she waved him off. "You know Charlie. Work first, then eat and relax. He'll be looking for something to gnaw on very soon." She glanced toward her mate.

Darren followed her gaze and looked toward the living room. His uncle was testing the recliner, a cold beverage in his hand, a baseball game already on the TV. He was uninterested in their conversation, seeking his own place of solace after being confined too closely for too many hours to his critically demeaning wife.

"Relax! We're on vacation," she urged with suggestion. She paused and leaned against the counter, the cupboard door still open where she was unloading. "Do you know where your sister is?" she inquired.

Darren did not withhold his smile. "Lost her already? I'm not surprised." He wondered on the suggestion of the question and what his responsibility might be.

"Oh, I know," Ethel smiled back and paused, looking toward the front door. "If you can," she paused again, "would you help me keep track of those two?" The question lingered like a fowl odor and Darren frowned, unable to hide his disapproval of the suggested assignment.

"No, no… don't worry, Hon," and she waved her hand again. "They're not your responsibility," she noted. "I can handle those two."

Darren looked around. The cooler had already been emptied and water pooled on the floor nearby. His cousins were out on the rear deck filling water balloons. He looked back at Ethel and she shrugged her shoulders in approval.

"Hey Darren," this time she used his name to get his full attention. "There's a concert tonight on the pier. Thought you and Deidra, and her friend of course, might want to go," she offered.

The concert began with the showing of a video. The music was full and intriguing. The singer had long greasy hair and wore a dingy t-shirt as he pounded on a hammered dulcimer. The small hammers moved so quickly they were a blur as he sang, *"…and I believe what I believe is what makes me what I am, I did not make it, no it is making me. It is the very truth of God and not the invention of any man…"* (partial lyrics from "Creed" by Rich Mullins, 1993: A Liturgy, A Legacy, and a Ragamuffin Band).

The differing words and style of music immediately caught Darren's attention. He watched and listened intently.

A young man came to the mic' and welcomed them to the Rich Mullins tribute concert. He looked similar in appearance, but dressed better, noting that he did not possess the talents of Mullins, but continues to be inspired and encouraged by the message of his lyrics. He described Rich Mullins as a deeply spiritual person.

Mullins was killed in a tragic highway accident on September 19, 1997 near Peroia, Illinois. He was 41 years old. It was as if the words of his song had set in motion the course of his end, as an anomalous paradox. He sang:

"The Jordan is waiting for me to cross through,

My heart is aging, I can tell.

So Lord, I'm begging,

For one last favor from You.

Here's my heart, take it where You will."

"This life has shown me how we're mended,

And how we're torn,

How it's okay to be lonely as long as you're free.

Sometimes my ground was stoney,

And sometimes covered up with thorns,

And only You could make it what it had to be,

And now that it's done..."

"Well, if they dressed me like a pauper,

Or if they dined me like a prince,

If they lay me with my fathers,

Or if my ashes scatter on the wind,

I don't care."

"But when I leave I want to go out like Elijah,

With a whirlwind to fuel my chariot of fire,

And when I look back on the stars,

Well, it'll be like a candlelight in Central Park,

And it won't break my heart to say goodbye."

(partial lyrics from "Elijah" by Rich Mullins, 1986: Songs).

Rich Mullins was thrown from a SUV after losing control of his vehicle as it flipped over. He was then struck by a tractor-trailer as its driver swerved to avoid crashing into the overturned car. The singer-song writer was on his way to a benefit concert in his hometown of Wichita, Kansas.

"But I believe the Savior was with him during that crash," the speaker noted. Yes, it was a whirlwind, and I believe he was taken into glory in his chariot of fire."

Darren was stunned at the proclamation. He looked to Deidra, teary eyed, and then Kyle, stone faced.

"The next song I want to sing he wrote in 1996. It is entitled, "We Are Not As Strong As We Think We Are." And he cooed:

"We are frail, we are fearfully and wonderfully made,

Forged in the fires of human passion,

Choking on the fumes of selfish rage."

"And with these, our hells and our heavens,

So few inches apart,

We must be awfully small,

And not as strong as we think we are."

71

(partial lyrics of "We Are Not As Strong As We Think We Are,"
by Rich Mullins, 1996: Songs. All credit to Rich Mullins Music, Inc.).

Darren was thinking about the threshold he had crossed, the gateway to adulthood. What should he do next? Should he join the Air Force?

The words of yet another song rattled in his brain.

"Why do the nations rage?

Why do they plot and scheme?

Their bullets can't stop the prayers we pray,

In the name of the Prince of Peace."

"We walk in faith and remember long ago,

How they killed Him and then how on the third day He arose,

Well, things may look bad,

And things my look grim,

But all these things must pass except the things that are of

Him."

(partial lyrics from "While the Nations Rage," by Rich Mullins, 1989: Never Picture Perfect. All credit to Rich Mullins Music, Inc.).

"Rich Mullins wrote nine new songs just nine days before he died," the young evangelist noted as he held up a CD album. "This is 'The Jesus Record.' It was released posthumously ten months after his death. It has the originals of the new songs, recorded on a simple tape-recorder in an abandoned church. Rich was planning a concept album based on the life of Jesus. He never completed it, but his band did."

"I love it!" he exclaimed. "And I have ten copies that I want to give away tonight. But more importantly," he urged, "I want to pray with anyone who is hearing God's voice tonight. Perhaps you are dealing with a difficulty or facing a new challenge. Whatever your need is, I'd be honored to pray with you. Come now, and the first ten will receive the new album."

A hush fell over the audience as a recording of Mullins began. Darren leaned toward his twin sister, sitting next to him. "Well, I'm struggling with my future," he noted. "Let's go down and meet this guy," he suggested reluctantly.

With glistening eyes, Deidra nodded in approval. Darren took her hand but she hesitated, remaining firm in her seat. She leaned toward Kyle and whispered into his ear.

"You go," she returned to tell Darren. "I think I'm going to pass." She looked away quickly. "I hope you get the CD," she offered in reconciliation, whispering a bit louder.

"Hey there you guys are," Aunt Ethel offered in greeting. "How was the concert?"

Kyle pushed by without acknowledging her and headed down the hallway. Deidra paused as she watched him pull away.

"I liked it," Darren offered enthusiastically. "Great music!"

"Tell me more," Ethel suggested as Deidra also left the room.

Darren related the story of the songwriter and his untimely death.

Minutes later, Deidra and Kyle suddenly popped into view with a quick announcement. "We're going for a walk on the beach," she informed.

"Yes, but don't be late," Ethel suggested. But then afraid she had just over stepped the delicate boundary that narrowly existed between them, she quickly interjected, "Be safe."

The couple left quickly without a reply.

The house was quiet when Darren stirred the next morning. Kyle's bed was empty, still neatly made. On his way to the refrigerator

Darren saw his sister sitting on the front deck. With a thump the sliding door gave way and a cool breeze touched his face, greeting him to a glorious dawn. The sky was an expanse of orange. Seagulls called as they floated by.

Deidra was sitting on a resin Adirondack chair, leaning back, and her feet propped up and resting on the railing.

"Mind if I join you?" Darren said softly, hoping not to impose. She simply smiled in return. He waited another moment and pulled up another chair. Neither spoke a word for several moments, feeling their bond as each sensed the thoughts of the other.

"Where's Kyle?" he broke the silence.

"Oh, he's taking a shower."

Darren looked at the brightening sky with cumulus clouds encroaching from the north. "Looks like it's going to be a nice day."

She was looking even farther away.

"You okay?" he probed.

"Oh yeah, I'm good," Deidra smiled and patted his hand.

There was silence again.

"Did you get the CD?" she asked quietly. It appeared that she wanted to talk about the concert they attended together the night before.

"Naw, I wasn't one of the first ones." And Darren reflected on the insightful lyrics once again. He had asked for a prayer for guidance.

"Kyle was a little put off," Deidra offered. "Guess I could say he was a little bit annoyed with all of it." She looked to her brother and he shrugged his shoulders.

"He invited me to go with him to his church when we get back," she continued. "It's some kind of orthodox religion," she paused. "I don't know…"

"Do they believe the same as we do?" Darren wondered aloud. "Are you comfortable with it?"

"Honestly, I don't think it really matters," Deidra said while gazing beyond. She turned to Darren and caught his eye. "I mean, god is god. All religion is basically the same," she explained.

Darren swallowed hard, surprised at the lack of commitment she expressed. "Really?" was all he could mouth in reply.

Deidra knew what his question implied. She appeared to be deep in thought and her twin brother wondered if she was going to let the question pass as rhetorical.

"There's some merit in believing," she reasoned. "I just don't think religion is that important to me." Her face contorted as she considered her next thought. "It's not helping mom."

"But Deidra," he objected and was immediately interrupted. She quickly stood, an empty coffee mug in her hand.

"Got to go, little brother," she said in tease. "My prince awaits." And with that she spun on her heels and walked away.

Hell's Revenge: "Progress to report," the demon Captains announce to their Major, the one specializing in false religion. "She is now yours."

Together they hiss gleefully as they review the plan. First there was anger, then denial with pleasure, and now false religion is taking root, distancing her from God and persuading her along their path of doom.

Heaven's Repose: "Stay close to her," the Intercessor tells his Holy Spirit, His Presence. "Speak to her of the great deception. Draw her to my Word. The Truth will set her free."

And the Savior commands his angels to guide and protect Darren in answer to his reverent and earnest prayers. He will stay close as a welcome companion as Darren makes plans for his future.

It was the day after Christmas, December 26, 2004. An undersea earthquake with a magnitude of 9.0 struck off the coast of

the Indonesian island of Sumatra. Within seven hours a wall of water reached across the Indian Ocean and devastated the coastal areas. Families were decimated and tourists were swept out into the sea. The tsunami killed up to 230,000 people in a dozen countries. Then, the lack of necessities such as food, clean water, and medical supplies increased the number of casualties.

2006:

On Saturday, December 30, Saddam Hussein is executed by hanging. He was convicted of crimes against humanity for the 148 Shi'ites he allegedly murdered in retaliation for an assassination attempt against him.

2011:

Osama bin Laden is shot and killed by U.S. Special Forces on May 2, during an early morning raid on his home in Pakistan. There was a $25 million reward for his capture, but no one received the bounty. The raid was the result of electronic intelligence, not the assistance of a human informant. Bin Laden was the infamous leader of Al Qaeda and believed to be instrumental in the 911 attacks against the U.S.

A New Islamic State

Muslims who pledged allegiance to Al Qaeda form a new Islamic state and claim religious, political, and military authority over all Muslims, worldwide. In America, the organization is acknowledged as the birth of "radical Islamic terrorism." In the Middle East it is first called, ISIS, Islamic State of Iraq and Syria, and later renamed as ISIL, Islamic State of Iraq and the Levant.

Although legitimate Muslim nations reject its statehood, ISIL quickly expands into 18 countries. It captures the attention of the world with its video beheadings of journalists and aid workers.

SECTION TWO

OUR DEMISE – the earth shakes violently. A

volcano erupts. The number of fatalities is tens of thousands in the United States.

Because lawlessness has increased, the love of many has waxed cold. Each cares only for their own rights.

Immediately following the simultaneous quakes of San Andreas and New Madrid, the country experiences great turmoil. The electrical grid fails on the eastern seaboard. Electricity is essential in aiding and supplying the population. As food supplies dwindle there is widespread rioting.

Having been the target of random killings and public disregard, the force responsible for law and order does not respond, but disbands. The fabric of society is ripped and the United States of America falls into anarchy. The U.S. government retreats and goes into hiding. Pandemonium spreads rapidly, from city to city, fanning outward into suburbia.

The calamity of the end of times begins with a distinct conflict among the world's greatest religions. Christianity immediately proclaims the judgment of God and the soon return of Jesus. Islam responds by blaming the followers of Christ for their moral decline, and crediting Allah with the intervention needed to redeem humanity. Zionists proclaim their independent righteous sovereignty as His chosen people and predict the imminent coming of their Messiah.

Jihadists, the radical Islamic enemies of the United States, seize the opportunity to occupy Washington D.C. and from there rush onward into the great cities of the north Atlantic region, the sacred places of the founding of the Republic. They open the gateway for an alliance of Muslim nations ISIL, to invade and conquer America, encountering little resistance.

The Republic is defeated and the Union of states in North America is dissolved.

Good men have lost their will to fight for freedom. The U.S. had declined morally until it was ripe for destruction.

The Islamic State of Iraq and the Levant increases its occupation and establishes a new order which soon is accepted by the citizens of discontent.

Initially, Americans are downtrodden, consumed by their losses, and without hope. As radicals establish their authority, they execute U.S. military operatives and Christian insurgents. It is a spontaneous killing in accordance with the edict of their righteous indignation.

The words of the Constitution are now without effect, a haunting echo from the past:

"We the People of the United States, in Order to form a more perfect Union, establish Justice, insure domestic Tranquility, provide for the common defense, promote the general Welfare, and secure the Blessings of Liberty to ourselves and our Posterity, do ordain and establish..."

Pages of the Qur'an are blowing with the fallen leaves. A Muslim nation has invaded a Christian nation.

Chapter 4

Pride is the power in rejecting God's call.

The greatest enemy lies within. Beware when an attitude of

entitlement takes root.

Selfish ambition provides fleeting success and an insatiable

appetite for more.

2012:

Darren is sitting erect in a swivel chair. His feet rest flat on a

raised platform as he sways gently from side to side. His seat is gimbal

mounted for free movement. He is wearing a helmet that includes

goggles and earphones. It has a black shield that wraps around the front

of his face, keeping him in complete isolation. Distractions to a pilot are

not allowed in this Ground Control Station, (GCS). He has the view off the nose of the drone he flies. The cross hairs of his weapon's firing mechanism are constantly in motion as he comes closer and closer to his target.

His view is three dimensional and in full color. He has virtual reality in this pilot program, operating the Peregrine prototype.

His forearms rest lightly on the arms of the chair with his hands extended beyond where he holds joy-stick controllers. One makes the drone turn abruptly; the other changes its elevation. Under his right thumb is the trigger that will launch the doomsday air-to-ground missile. The switch under his left thumb surrenders the aircraft to autopilot for a fast retreat with an instant gain of altitude. The drone is now about 100 feet above the ground. His hands are sweaty.

The mood is tense in this small room, isolated in the basement of a military installation known only to those with a highest security clearance.

What Darren sees is also visible to another young man, sitting at a computer terminal. Yet another monitor gives the satellite view to a third person on the team. Today, it is a woman. This view will be used for verification of a hit.

He gets closer to the target, a Muslim man walking with three others in a narrow street. Darren knows that he must hold steady for at least a second, a fraction before firing and a fraction of a second after pulling the trigger. He will then press the button in his left hand, giving control to his comrade, and co-pilot. He also knows that he must fire within a range of 500 to 300 feet of his target, or retreat and likely abort the mission. The distance to the target is indicated by numbers rapidly declining, seen in the top left of his view. "Can you slow me down?" he instructs.

Watching from behind, through a large window, are several of his ranking officers. This is a top-secret mission with a specific directive. This is their chance to kill another terrorist on the most wanted list.

It's better than any video game he has ever played. Darren feels a great responsibility at this moment, but is not nervous, confident in this gaming atmosphere. Some days the shoot is real, other times it is merely a training exercise. The pilot is not told beforehand which it will be. Darren is unaware of the spectators behind him.

He presses the red trigger button as he squeezes his right hand, then the left, and sees a flash of light in the bottom of his view. He relaxes his posture and leans back. Before his eyes is the azure of the cloudless sky.

•

He feels someone nudge his shoulder before removing his helmet. The Peregrine is on its way back to the base, safe and sound. The target has been terminated in an explosion of fiery hell.

Darren pulls off his helmet to see his co-pilots smiling ear to ear. "You got him buddy. Great job!" The other confirms, "That was real nice flying, Darren." There are high fives all around. Darren glances at the satellite view. A building is burning. Within the block there are people running, some toward the explosion, others away from it.

There is a knock on the glass window. Darren turns around to see thumbs up from his commanding officer. Everyone is jovial.

He was believed to be al Qaeda's most senior leader in Pakistan. On February 9, 2012, Badar Mansoor was killed by similar technology, a missile launched from a U.S. drone. The leader of 200 radical fighters, there was a $5 million bounty on his head.

The land is flat and the scenery is boring. Darren is beginning to nod at the wheel of his 2011 Jeep Wrangler, the 4-door model with a soft top. The sun glistens off the hood, brownish orange in color, as it flashes in his eyes and pricks at consciousness. He is headed home with mixed feelings and some anxiety.

Towering at 6'1" he is buff and well toned, handsome in his military haircut, sandy blonde on top. Following five years of college, Darren enlisted with the Air Force. Way behind him now is Hill AFB of Layton, Utah, and the snow banks of Park City. He completed training on UCAV's, Unmanned Combat Aerial Vehicles, at Creech. His dear friend, Jason Peterson, had transferred from Nevada to Utah and Darren couldn't pass up the opportunity of a visit while traveling back east. He is headed for an undisclosed location in Virginia on a classified mission. He suspects there is a new GCS located there, the next phase of the Peregrine CIM (Combative In Motion) program. Darren is experienced in flying the MQ-1 Predator, with several important hits already to his credit, qualifying him for the advancement.

All he sees now in his rear view mirror while racing through Nebraska are dried up corn fields. Like the ruins of war, they remain, waiting to be plowed under in hope of a new and productive year, shielded in peace. Due to a pressing drought that year, many farmers did not even attempt a harvest. An hour out of Lincoln, he still has twelve hours to go.

The challenges of life come like the struggle the battalion faces while charging into battle. Some soldiers will live and others will die.

Their destiny is determined by training, personal ability, the choices they make, and providence. But what has the survivor learned?

Some become stronger; others are weakened. Some advance to greater conflicts; others retreat in life. Some become self-reliant; others dependent on a power greater than themselves.

In the battlefield of life, Deidra and Darren are becoming two different kinds of soldiers. Darren is beginning to understand that his life is more than physical, but also has an intriguing spiritual component. He is becoming more reliant on God.

A family dinner is set for tomorrow, Saturday evening, with Aunt Ethel and Uncle Charlie. His mother is invited, but not expected. Terry has been recently disabled with multiple sclerosis, and seldom ventures out of her refuge of reclusion. Darren will drop in to visit his Mom next week, even if she objects.

He feels melancholy rising in his heart. It comes with the thought of her being alone and tormented by her past. She is sitting in a darkened apartment. It is disheveled and dirty. She is unkempt. Her eyes appear to be glossed over. Her responses are delayed.

"God, please help my mom today," Darren quickly prays to ease his conscience. "May she know your healing peace. Protect and help her, I pray in Jesus name, amen."

And just then his cell phone tones and vibrates. He has received a text from his twin sister.

"I will arrive in Bloomington in about 3 hours. Can't wait to see you!"

Since the summer of '04, when they went different ways, time passed quickly, and with each ensuing year, it seemed that their visits were less, and less frequent. Darren thought back to New Year's Day when he last saw his twin sister. It had been almost a year.

His phone alerts him again. "Can we meet tonight. Maybe at the Deli, about 7?"

Darren presses the microphone symbol to reply. "Can't. I get in late. How about breakfast?"

"It's a date."

After high school Deidra attended George Washington University, desiring to feel the pulse of the nation. She achieved a Bachelor of Arts Degree with a major in political science. She was

accepted into graduate school and earned her Master's Degree,
specializing in Public Policy and Administration. Currently, she lives in
Columbus, Ohio, and works for a state senator, running his re-election
campaign and representing him at meetings he cannot or will not attend,
handling the media like a seasoned pro. This year she ran for delegate
and was elected to attend the Democratic National Convention, held in
September in Charlotte. The recent memory of Thursday, September 6,
as Barack Obama accepted the nomination to run for his second term as
President of the United States is still fresh in her mind.

Darren yanked hard on the door handle and jarred himself before
seeing the "PUSH" sign. Feeling a little embarrassed, he straightened his
cap in an effort to regain his composure, hoping that no one had seen his
fool-hardy display. But she had. There she stood with a broad smile on
her face, her teeth whiter than fresh fallen snow.

He expected to see a young man standing alongside, as Deidra
had had many male friends and seldom travelled alone. But there she
stood, all alone, and beautiful as ever. She wore ankle high boots with
three inch heels, tight jeans, and a thin coat, fitted at the waist and open
above its enclosure there. Her hair was blonde and flowed gently over
the faux fur trim of the wide collar that highlighted the red jacket. Its

purpose was obviously fashion, not warmth. Deidra often lightened her hair as it contrasted her dark blue eyes, always wonting with an intimate desire that only she could manage as lethal against an unwanted aggressor emboldened by her appearance to make a pass.

She was the model "Barbie," always worth a second glance, often from the wandering eyes of the married man.

She quickly stepped forward and with a chuckle pulled her twin brother in for a tight hug. She looked into his eyes and seeing herself, she placed a kiss firmly on his lips, and then checked for affirmation. He was smiling, ear to ear.

After sliding onto the benches of a booth facing each other, he quickly probed. "Hey Sis, are you alone?"

"Never… really," she teased. "How about you, little brother? No adoring little lady for you?"

They both laughed, feeling the connection of their birth and early years, enjoying the intensity of their reunion until interrupted by a waitress.

"I'm too busy right now for a relationship," she offered, after ordering coffee, black, and toast, dry, with a glass of water. "Men are so demanding, and such whiners," she smiled to appease him. "But not you, of course," she concurred.

"Wow! Look at you. A Navy man," she continued with genuine adoration. "God bless America!"

Forty-five minutes later they stood side by side in front of the restaurant. She reached around his waist and pulled him close. For a moment he nuzzled in the crook of her neck, like he did when he was a little boy. She kissed his ear and said pleadingly, "Darren, don't ever give up on me."

He looked into her eyes with confusion in his.

"I hadn't heard from you for such a long time," she explained.

"I'm sorry Deidra," he countered. "It's the military. Always got you on the run."

"I know you're busy," she said with tears welling into the corners of her eyes. "You and me," she suggested with a shrug of her shoulders. "We will always be one."

They embraced and promised to see each other more often.

"Bye," he said, releasing her hand.

"No! Never goodbye!" she retorted. She grasped his hand and squeezed it firmly, causing him to reconsider.

He turned to face her squarely. "Deidra, are you okay?" He paused and looked deep into her eyes. "Is there anything I need to know?"

"Heck, no!" She waved her hand in the air as if pushing his concern away. "You're the sensitive one. I'm the toughie. But look at us now. We've switched and taken each other's place."

"You sure?" he asked, prying deeper.

"Just no goodbyes. Okay?" her voice quivered and she released his hand.

"Then see ya," he offered. "See ya soon!"

She smiled and stepped away. Pausing she turned back and said, "That's right. Yeah… tomorrow I expect."

Uncle Charlie seemed a bit agitated. Deidra was back on her game and tried to eavesdrop on his conversation with Darren as they stood in the archway entrance to the living room.

"But why do you want a gun now?" Darren was asking. "If you've never owned one before, then why now?"

"My neighbor's house was broken into recently," Charlie explained. "There are more break-ins, but beyond that it seems like civil unrest is increasing."

"What do you mean?"

"Well, look at that shooting in the movie theater," Charlie moaned.

"Are you going to carry?" Darren persisted.

"Perhaps, eventually. We need protection!"

Darren was surprised at the proclamation and looked toward the dining room and kitchen hoping to find an exhibition of civility and calm. Deidra acknowledged their talk with a raised eyebrow.

"You heard about Topeka?" Charlie probed. After waiting a few seconds for an answer, he continued, "two police officers gunned down."

Ethel suddenly appeared in the dining room with a platter in her hands. Steam was rising from the sliced pork. "Com' on boys," she interrupted. "Let's eat."

"So what would you recommend," Charlie was persisting, "for home defense?" He was thinking about the ad he saw yesterday for a gun show to be held at a local fire hall next month.

"A shot gun is good for home defense," Darren reasoned. "Maybe a Persuader," he suggested. "It is pump action and holds six rounds. You shoot from the hip, usually at close range. It can do a lot of damage."

"Com' on, come on! Let's eat while it's still hot," Ethel was urging with some impatience.

There was a short prayer and bowls were passed quickly.

"Daddy, you gettin' a gun?" Alana, now 13 years old, broke the silence.

Surprised by the question, he quickly swallowed a partially chewed piece of pork and choked on it. He grabbed for a glass of water and quickly washed it down.

"Thinking about it," he whined as he tried to clear his throat. "Shawn and I may take up hunting."

"Really?" Deidra injected.

"Well, I think a person should be able to protect their home," he offered more truthfully.

Deidra smiled confidently. "We have a Castle Law, and sure, that is within your right," she offered. "But it can be a tricky defense for the shooter, even when there is a home invasion."

Charlie was looking at his plate.

"If the intruder is unarmed," she suggested, "would you still shoot him?"

"And why can't you depend on the police?"

The mood was now tense. Charlie looked to his wife who had her disapproval expression prominently displayed.

"Okay, everyone," Ethel suggested. "Let's talk about something more pleasant."

"Do you think Obama will outlaw assault rifles?" Charlie shot a quick question toward his niece. "Or worse yet, will they try to take guns away from all of the good, law-abiding citizens?" he sneered at his wife.

Deidra was busy chewing on a large mouth full and quickly sat her fork on the table.

"The Democrats seem to be against guns," Darren urgently took the stage. "Remember the President's comment about people in the Midwest clinging to guns or religion?" he suggested. "Like they are less of a person for doing so…" he suggested.

"We all need God in our lives," Charlie stated with firm conviction. "Guns may be optional, but God… we truly need Him."

"Well okay," Deidra found her voice again, "but wait a minute. The DNC (Democratic National Committee) has taken a position against assault rifles like the AK-47 and AR-15. I agree. Why does anyone need one?" she stated as a foregone conclusion.

The discussion was becoming uncomfortable for everyone. But Deidra feeling a little bit riled up, continued, "Right now I don't need guns, or religion imposed upon me."

Charlie gasped and Darren sighed with an expectant understanding of her announcement. He looked into her eyes pleadingly, hoping she would promptly end her dissertation. But she continued.

"I really don't need God, or anyone else, for that matter. I'm doing just fine on my own." She cleared her throat in response to the restricted airway that came with the tension of knowing she was likely offending her relatives. "Don't get me wrong," she explained, "I believe, and I am a Christian. But religion is just not that important to me!"

"Le..le… let's," Ethel forced the word out after stuttering on it. "Let's have a nice time together. No more talk about guns," she paused, "politics or religion," she demanded. "We are family, and we will love and support each other," she was now soap-boxing, "despite differences in opinion," she paused, "on matters that are less important," she swallowed hard in interruption as she now suspected that she may have overstepped the invisible boundary of her position, especially with her husband, "than our being family and loving each other."

Her mini-lecture was effective in producing an immediate silence. Everyone stayed at the table and seemed to be content with the reprieve, an immediate cease fire determined to prevent the escalation of a conflict.

Charlie asked for someone to pass the potatoes. Deidra stretched to reach the bowl and handed it toward her uncle with a big smile, purposed at disarming him. It was successful, as her charm always was.

"Deidra," Ethel suggested. "I heard that you were in Washington D.C. for the inauguration. Tell me, was it as glamorous…?"

"Like I heard it was," she added. Ethel intended for the diversion to be a slide away from the controversies and hoped secretly that her question would now promote a safer discussion

Deidra's thoughts shifted from guns and God to parades, celebration, and pomp.

"Oh, you must mean the convention," she corrected her aunt. "I was elected as a delegate for Ohio. That was a great experience."

She paused. "But yes, I was able to attend the inauguration after Obama's first election in 2008."

Darren looked at his sister and smiled, realizing that the diversion was successful. He knows her to be a determined solider, unrelenting in a struggle. Her battlefield is the political arena.

It was a sunny day on January 20, 2009, when Deidra Daniels stood in a massive crowd of nearly 1.8 million people. They came to the nation's capitol to witness the inauguration of the 44th President of the United States of America. From her vantage point, she had Barack Obama within view. His words echoed over the crowd and few noticed the unintentional stumble of the President's oath. It was a glorious moment, indelibly engraved in her memory to be felt again and again, stirring her emotions repeatedly, for the rest of her days.

Few spectators knew that they were potentially standing there in harm's way. There was at that time a viable bomb threat known by intelligence officials based on information that radical Islamists from Somalia had entered the U.S. via Canada and intended to disrupt the ceremonies.

The Secretary of Homeland Security, Michael Chertoff, continued to quietly work behind the scenes to mitigate the threat, striving beyond the time upon which he would traditionally resign his post with the Bush administration and turn over the responsibilities of his office to the new, incoming Secretary, Janet Napolitano. Chertoff had the inauguration event designated as a "National Special Security Event," allowing him exceptional privilege. He held his position until 12:01 the following day.

The police presence in D.C. was doubled, augmented by an additional 8,000 police officers from around the country. The FBI provided 1,000 agents to assist with security. Secret Service Counter-sniper teams were placed in hidden locations nearby. The National Guard was also on hand as 10,000 troops assisted with security and crowd control.

Secretary of Defense Robert Gates, chosen as the designated survivor, was held at a military installation outside of the capitol.

The inauguration ceremony and events continued as planned, without serious disturbance.

That evening everyone seemed to settle down. Charlie suggested to Darren that they should continue their conversation in private. They then quickly turned their banter to sports, primarily football, with an important game about to start as the pro's got closer to the playoffs.

The girls were in the kitchen filling the refrigerator with leftovers and spraying the dirty dishes. Deidra was probing on Larissa, wanting to hear about her senior prom and her latest boyfriend. Alana would interrupt with "classified" information intended to embarrass her older sister.

Shawn was looking for the remote, wanting to see the start of the game.

Charlie and Darren went to the garage, apparently to diagnose a problem with Charlie's old Ford pickup.

"Hey guys," Ethel shouted. "You have to see this." The college game was interrupted for a special news bulletin.

The prerecorded picture displayed crowds of angry parents held behind a police barricade. Some were shouting; others were crying. Panicked parents were demanding to be reunited with their young children.

The Sandy Hook Elementary School in Newtown, Connecticut was the scene of a shooting that occurred there on December 14. It would soon shock the country and the world to learn that Adam Lanza, 20, had fatally shot twenty young students between the ages of six and seven. He also murdered six adult staff members at the school.

Hell's Revenge: In the spiritual realm occupied by the agents of evil the mood is one of glee and it appears that an impromptu celebration of sorts is about to break out, but anger and hatred dominate. "We have her now," the demonic colonel of pride reports to his superior officer. "She is blinded by selfish ambition and has expressed great confidence in rejecting Yahweh."

"Don't say his name," the Brigadier General of self-sufficiency growls. "I know who we are battling against."

"Tell her more lies of entitlement. Fuel the fires of discontent," he commands. "This will better prepare her for me."

Heaven's Repose: Jesus weeps. The tragedy rips at his compassionate heart. In his human suffering he knew and now fully understands the catastrophe others are experiencing on earth.

"We must give reassurance and hope," the Savior commands the Spirit. "Move among my messengers who are true. Arouse their faith and stir them with compassion. Provide the Peace that Passes Understanding."

"This pain caused by evil will not endure!" the Messiah proclaims.

"Protect the faithful," he commands his legions of angels. "The time of divine intervention draweth nigh."

Charlie and his son Shawn are walking briskly along the slippery surface of a melting dirt parking lot. Charlie spent hours awake the night before. Today he is afraid of his intention of becoming a gun owner, fearing it may be a slippery slope into serious trouble.

The sun is shining brightly and this January day may break the record for a high temperature. He wonders about the extremes of weather and his new concern about massive, threatening storms. They are no longer such an oddity. It seems that the 100 year storm is coming every other month. There is no assurance that tomorrow won't bring a natural disaster, and a prolonged power outage.

The issues of safety and security are pressing heavily on his mind today. And Shawn, on the other hand, is almost too interested in the prospect of guns coming into their home. His father is suspicious that this may be an unhealthy interest. His memory is telling him of friends killed by accidental discharges while handling firearms.

Last night he saw a movie that sparked his interest. It helped him see a way through the fog of confusion about gun ownership.

A man consumed in a fit of rage for revenge had taken his recently acquired handgun and raced to the home of a locksmith who did not secure the front door to his grocery store after being hired to do so.

This neighborhood market was this immigrant's only hope for establishing himself in America. The locksmith said the door needed to be repaired. The owner suspected that he was being overcharged and taken advantage of once again. That night vandals came in and ransacked the store, destroying most of his merchandise. Because the locksmith had left a bill with a hand written note, the insurance company determined the loss to be the result of negligence and refused to reimburse. The note said that the door could not be secured by a lock and that the owner was advised to make repairs.

The store owner found the locksmith's address on the bill of sale. As he approached his house he began yelling. The locksmith went outside and an argument ensued.

Inside, a little girl becomes frightened and runs to her daddy. Just as she steps in front of him the angry man fires his gun.

It appears that the little girl has been killed in a terrible accident, the result of a misunderstanding fueled by the skepticism of cultural distrust. But just then she lifts her head to look at her father.

The gun had unknowingly been loaded with blanks, another mistake that was the result of a miscommunication caused by racial tension as it permeated the time of the gun's purchase.

The storekeeper drops to the sidewalk, crying in relief. His mood has suddenly changed. He is spared a tragedy despite his fit of rage.

Charlie struggled with the questions: is he willing to shoot an intruder in his home and can he accept the consequence of killing another person? And just then the haze of uncertainty and fear revisited him. He would be justified in self defense. He'd be smart to save his life and heroic to protect his family.

But what if he could scare the intruder into a quick retreat – wouldn't that be much better? It's often said that an intruder will stop whatever nefarious deed he's doing and flee at the sound of a shotgun merely being pumped. Better than that, Charlie reasoned, he could fire a blank at close range. *"Get out, or I'll blast your head off,"* he role played in his mind. *"The next shot will waste you."* Although more likely, the next shot would be rock salt. He had been reading about less than lethal rounds.

And, there are also flame throwers, the "Dragon's Breath," sure to be a big hit when the boys go out target shooting.

Despite the sunshine upon his face, the fog of doubt had still not lifted. But just then, his lack of confidence was reinforced by the determined looks on the faces of others. Some looked like businessmen.

Some wore long beards, unkempt like that of a hermit. Some were women. The line waiting to pay the admission price to the Eagle's Gun Club Gun Show was getting longer by the second. The aisles inside were becoming crowded.

"Please excuse me for asking," Charlie said to the dealer. "I have never owned a gun before." The stocky white-haired main wearing a hunter's vest was holding a rifle that looked like a military assault weapon, but it was mostly made of plastic, except for the barrel. He removed the magazine before showing it to his customer.

The dealer was patient in answering obvious questions for more than ten minutes, then sat the gun back down on the display table and started looking for a buying customer. Shawn had drifted off to a vendor of beef jerky, hoping for a sample. Charlie pressed on his thoughts, expecting the fog to clear with a view of the right direction to take.

It was now, or probably never. He had come this far.

"Okay, I'll take it," he shouted in the direction of the retreating dealer. After filling out a form and answering a long list of questions about citizenship and his criminal record, which was non-existent, he was handed the weapon. Charlie had joined the ranks of his fellow Americans determined to exercise their Second Amendment rights. He would stand with them in defense of his home and community.

In the U.S. gun sales are soaring. In 2015 records maintained in accordance with the National Firearms Act indicate an increase of gun transfers that is nearly ten times what it was in 2005. The number of transactions involving firearms increased from 147 thousand to 1.4 million.

Chapter 5

I have read a fiery gospel writ in burnish'd rows of steel,

Self sufficiency provides a sense of security that makes one unresponsive to conviction.

Years later, sometime in the near future:

And the earth shook violently!

April 1:

It was the first of April, fools day, nearly 5 pm central time. Charlie was commuting home from work. He was listening to the car radio when the emergency broadcast system interrupted his oldie from the eighties. Earthquakes had struck the United States of America. Citizens were advised to "shelter at home," and wait for further instructions.

Charlie placed a quick call to Ethel. Yes, she was home and so were the kids, except for Larissa, who had already called, having been sent home from her desk at the customer call center. The lights blinked and Shawn was complaining about losing his place in the computer game he was playing. The house had shaken lightly but there was no obvious damage. Ethel demanded to know what was happening. Charlie couldn't say, but instructed her to keep the kids in the house and to go to the local grocery store. "Stock up on non-perishables and paper products," he instructed. "No meats, no dairy, no frozen, nothing that needs to be refrigerated," he elaborated. "Get going. Do it quick." He paused and then asked, "Do we have a good can opener?"

Ethel objected. "I just bought groceries! What are you talking about?"

"Please, just go, and do it. A surplus of canned goods can't hurt us."

"But I spent our food budget for this week," she persisted, and paused. The lights blinked again and the hum of the refrigerator was distinctive as it restarted. Fear began to creep into her mind. Ethel reached for the edge of the countertop as she felt a vibration under her feet. It was an aftershock. She opened the pantry door and thought about eating out of cans, uncooked food. *"Yuck!"* The lights blinked again, twice, and then went out. She reached for the flashlight kept on the top shelf, hoping it was still there behind the boxes of cake mix. There wasn't much here to sustain a family of five.

Suddenly, in the dim light of dusk, she had an eerie feeling, with chills on her spine - the threat of what was coming, although still unknown to her. Soon it would be dark. She had to get ahold of herself – and not let her imagination take control.

The cold of night is near, but the promise of a new day dawning, despite the dreary forecast of rain, gives her some reprieve. But what of tomorrow? And the next day? And the next?

What if the power is not restored? Could it be real – the doomsday scenario Charlie is always whining about? He seemed to be so negative as of late.

The sun drops quickly behind the western horizon. The darkness of uncertainty, and yes, even fear, penetrates her psychological state as shadows begin to creep in.

"Charlie, are you still there?" she asks. "I'm going."

"Thanks hon. I'll be home soon." And just then Charlie decides to stop at the supermarket along his route and do some additional shopping. He needs batteries for his flashlights and radio, double AA, and a 9 volt. "Don't worry. We'll be okay." He is already thinking about the locations of his shotgun, the locked ammunition box, and the key hidden in his desk.

As Ethel approached the local market, she could hear the hum of their generator, located at the rear of the building. The store was crowded and a feeling of panic permeated the air thick with apprehension. At the cash register she overheard the manager giving instructions to close the store.

Deidra was still sitting in her cubical in an office building in Columbus at 5 pm. The eighth floor of her building swayed gently. Stunned by the movement, she instinctively grabbed at the edge of her desk. A bobble-head of Barack Obama was nodding at her with false assurance.

She looked at the email she was writing to her new boss, still displayed on her computer screen. Deidra had accepted a new job with the Democratic National Committee and was finalizing the details of her move to Washington D.C.

Her new supervisor had already peppered Deidra with questions about her abilities and intentions as she contemplated her new aide's first assignment.

"I am confident in my ability, based on my extensive experience and determination…" The sentence Deidra was writing in reply remained incomplete due to the interruption.

The lights blinked. Her computer made a clicking sound and the monitor re-lighted with the manufacturer's logo. There was a unanimous groveling of complaint aired in monotone from her colleagues in the large room, others working late in hopes of also ascending the ladder of success. The monitor blinked twice and her email program restarted. Now she was looking at her inbox. Her message was gone, unless saved automatically in the draft folder.

Deidra was anxious to leave Ohio and arrive in D.C. Her bags were already packed. The moving truck had left her apartment earlier that afternoon. This was to be her last night in Columbus, staying with a friend, at his place. She had planned for a short romantic interlude, an endearing goodbye, with no intention of reuniting with Bill in the foreseeable future.

Now, she is still determined to leave in the morning. This new job represents the big break she has been working for, for many years.

"I've got to get there and claim my turf, before anything happens," she tells herself. *"Maybe I should start the trip right now…"*

She hits the power button and looks to the pasteboard box sitting on the floor alongside her desk chair. It contains a few framed photos and a few folders, all personal items that belong to her exclusively.

She reaches for the bobble head and drops it into the container.

The lights blinked again and then went out. She glanced toward the orange glow outside the large office windows, previously unnoticed. It was a remarkable sunset, a panoramic of vivid color. Deidra felt only confidence, undisturbed by the suggestions of a disastrous event, completely sustained in her self-sufficiency that was well established by the fortress of determined successes, upon which she built her life.

There was another humming noise and the lights came back on, powered by the building's emergency generator.

Yes, she would leave now. Columbus was already in her rear view mirror as she was blinded by the brilliant light of opportunity in the majestic Land of Oz. It lay just ahead, within view, on the horizon, just a little further, along the yellow brick road.

His name is William Bates, an aspiring environmental engineer working for the state with a promising future. She would call Bill from the road, after leaving the city and entering the open road of the interstate highway. Yes, he would be disappointed, but she cared little. Most likely, her call would go to his voicemail, as he seldom answered.

Deidra was blinded by ambition, and already addicted to an expectation of achievement. The excitement of the pulse and power of the nation's capitol was calling her name, resounding in her ears even now.

Surely emergency management was prepared for whatever might be happening. It would be better for her to be there, she reasoned, among other important people, entitled and properly protected.

Six months prior to the quake, Barbara Daniels moved into a village for the retired. She had hung onto the family homestead in Detroit as long as she could. But it needed repairs: paint and plumbing fixes. When the furnace stopped working on that frosty October night and she had trouble getting a repairman to come quickly, she finalized in her mind the difficult decision to sell the place, half a duplex that she had owned with her husband Fred. It had been their modest family home.

A dark cloud of remorse hung over her with that decision. She knew that Ethel, her daughter, was doing well, and she enjoyed the company of her grandchildren on occasion, although their visits were becoming fewer with each year, and the time between them even greater.

After all, the kids were grown up now. She seldom saw Deidra or Darren, both busy with their ambitious careers.

The move to Joliet, a suburb of Chicago, placed her closer to the Sworsens. Ethel had strongly recommended the change.

Many years had passed since Fred had died suddenly, and this widow thought of him frequently, still feeling the loss that was unrelenting upon her heart.

Perhaps it was just age. She was living in the time of waning light, the twilight of her life, nightfall without the colors of a joyful sunset, the motion of time increasing with greater personal decline and loss.

Living alone, she had struggled with the thoughts of her end. Regret, primarily.

With the plan finalized to move, she was determined not to give it any more consideration. She would make new friends and busy herself with petty concerns, while living among others her age, cared for by a business entity. She must trust the institution, despite her misgivings of doubt.

She acquired a small flat with a studio apartment on the ground floor. Her social security checks covered her rental fees. She opted for little else, none of the accessory benefits offered at the village, except for a meager dinner meal each evening. It was required.

Her front door opened to a pretty walkway lined with flowers. It led to an atrium from whence other walkways went off in angles, like the spokes of a wheel, leading to other suites of meager size and accommodation. A wider pathway led to the main building that contained the huge lobby, dining room, and small spaces down dark hallways for those requiring nursing care. Barbara preferred not to visit there.

Today she wondered about her son, Joseph. She had received an unusual and unexpected letter, brief as it was, from him about three months ago. It was like the ray of sunshine after a thunder storm, piercing upon the wet earth with undisputable proof of a silver lining, a glimmering of hope.

She had long ago given up on him. She had relinquished any desire of ever hearing from Joseph again. She made a quick reply to his note, and then faced another void of communication, dead space that hurt her deeply, as her renewed hope of a reunion withered with each passing day that she encountered an empty mailbox. The pain of losing others returned with vengeance. Gloom clouded out any wanting of her remaining years, or days, the distinction upon which she had little preference.

She felt that there was something unusual about that day, the day of the earthquake. Most others in the facility made no notice of it. The chandelier in the lobby swayed back and forth, casting unusual shadows upon the counter in the reception area. Employees and nurses began chattering incessantly to each other in huddles not allowed by their supervisors. Many were immediately looking at their smart phones. Those alive enough to be aware of the shaking, or to care, turned on their television sets. The newscast echoed in the atrium and the light of their liquid crystal displays blinked in unison, the affect like the flickering of an old movie. But this show brought only bad news.

Then the lights went out, along with their TVs, and everyone gasped, like the dying, starving for oxygen.

But the end had not yet come to all who inhabited this warehouse of the aged. Two corpses had been pushed out of the rear door on a gurney earlier that very day. The grim reaper had made his quota.

It was an occurrence upon which the other residents were well acquainted, and accepted, in a void of hope: their life's light already dimmed.

Above, the doorways exit signs and their beams of precarious illumination responded immediately, operated by batteries. A long minute passed and then the elderly home groaned from its bowels as a diesel powered generator rattled and began producing electricity for the needy facility.

A single man stands on the sidewalk as the ground under his feet quivers. A traffic light nearby is swinging precariously on its line. This catches his attention as he waits for the pedestrian signal at an intersection of potholed roads in the deteriorated city of Detroit.

What he sees is a ghost of better times, when the auto industry thrived there, many decades ago. Truly, the city has died. It is now ridden with crime.

He stands six feet tall, is stocky and well built, erect with an exhibition of strength while surefooted, like a tall building constructed on a firm foundation of impenetrable concrete and steel. Inside, this man is a fortress of strength and durability, unwavering, almost untouchable. Times of war, relentless training with demands for greater personal sacrifice and mental determination, physical exercises that were torture at first but then became a pinnacle of prowess, and many long years of survival in conditions wanting of even the basic necessities, made Joseph

Daniels a veteran of great strength. He is tough in all ways, except those emotional. He lost feelings for others, and himself, in those early years of his abandonment.

It is debatable – if that part of his brain had died. More likely, it was reprogrammed with the intensity of the determinations needed to kill the enemy, consumed with the skills of survival in the face of extreme opposition. This is the force that consumed him. This is the life of a career soldier during the time of war, one who served during the American conflicts with Muslim nations in the Middle East.

Upon retiring from the Marine Corps, Daniels had acquired the rank of First Sergeant, E-8. He proudly wore the scars of seven tours, having been deployed in Iraq, Afghanistan, Kuwait, and Yemen.

Today he is wearing green cargo pants, military grade, covering over the tops of his high, black polished boots, laced through their many eyelets.

Just putting on these boots requires a chore which the undisciplined, belly fat civilians are unwilling to endure. Even attempting to do so will choke off their airways and cause them to faint in exhaustion. This footwear represents determination, and honor in its reflective shine - uncompromising in every way. This is a symbol of the Marine's creed.

Joseph is unbothered by the chill in the air. His v-neck t-shirt is nude tan in color. His hair is cropped short, standing erect above his forehead. His jaw is square and its muscles bulge from clenched teeth; his eyes are light hazel in color, dim like the bulb of a flashlight powered by depleted batteries, indicative of the spirit convalescing inside. Bare skin is visible above his ears, deeply tanned.

His movements are quick and exact, as if pre-calculated by previous maneuvers. He has four blocks to walk before arriving at 36 Ridge Drive, his childhood home. He instinctively looks at his wrist watch. He has mentally documented the time of the quake.

Standing in front of the house he is at first stunned and then dazed. His mind is reeling with disturbing memories from his past and unwelcome realities of these new determinations. The home is vacant, ghastly in abandonment. The front yard is full of weeds, highlighted by the garbage discarded there by passersby. The front porch is sagging. The structure is forlorn with the loss of humanity, the decline of the Daniels family. This is his heritage, his legacy. He wonders what his father must be thinking about this hideous display.

The realtor's sign is bent over, almost hidden by the over-growth.

He sees in his mind's eye the swing set in the backyard. He hears his mother calling to him and his sister. It is dinner time. He is anxious to see his father and ask for a new BB gun.

Next he sees himself as he parks his car a block down the street, out of his father's view from his vantage point through the front parlor window. Terry is sitting on the bench seat next to him. He knows better than to reach for her here. The neighbors will buzz with gossip. He is coaxing her to sit with him on the front porch swing. She doesn't want to encounter his parents. She is embarrassed by the late hour of their return. She wants to go home.

With his hands in his pocket, he feels fists forming instinctively. He is angry about his life. He regrets his decision to run like a scared rabbit. But once free, why did he come back? The past has always haunted him. He despises it.

He wishes that he had gone to a remote beach, somewhere on the Red Sea, in a foreign land, perhaps Dubai. He wonders why – why was he never able to love another? But how could he, all the while hating himself, still wondering about his unborn child.

He doubts that he has the fortitude required to fully face this remorseful past, or for finding his mother. A war is raging inside. His ears are ringing with the sounds of the explosions on the battlefield, and then the street light goes dark, as if it has been hit by a missile. His reflexes demand that he spin around to access the threat. He is expecting to be impacted by shattered glass. The ravages of his war endure.

Feelings of discontent are now the prevalent human emotion in America. Everyone is unfulfilled and unhappy, either by decline or in advancement to greater demands. Members of the Daniels family - their stressors are about to increase dramatically. Darren is now the most stable. But each has a mild form of dystopia even before encountering the imminent hardships that will mark the demise of their country, changing their lives forever. A totalitarian government is coming, from the east, already on the horizon and exposed by the prophesy of the rising sun.

April 2:

Darren is behind the wheel of his Jeep, beginning the descent from a three-mile high summit in northern Virginia. The valley is clearly seen below, lit by the town that grew rapidly at the outskirts of the suburban area populated by commuters to D.C. On this clear night the town glistens below like the stars above. It is 7 pm on the east coast and already dark.

Darren is upset about the news from the day before, the news of the first earthquake near San Francisco, and then another, within hours, near Memphis. He stayed up half the night listening to the newscasts. Still not fully accessed, the property damage is astronomical, and the death toll is steadily rising. There is huge infrastructure damage to many major cities. Millions of people are instantly without power, water, and heat. Tens of thousands need to be rescued. The entire country is in massive turmoil.

He was glad to go to work that morning, for a distraction, some temporary relief from the grief that overwhelmed him. Once through the security gates and within the concrete compound, the chaos of the world seems more like an imagined event, like a bad dream. Is it really happening?

He parked in an underground garage.

Here he is removed from natural surroundings. Here he is consumed by the concentration required for the mission.

Darren sees a shooting star arc over the valley below. He wonders what the thoughts of the Creator are. Surely He feels the plight of humanity as He sits on His majestic throne and observes the mayhem on earth below. Darren decides to trust in His sovereignty, much as Abraham Lincoln believed in providence during the great conflict documented by history as the Civil War. It was the bloodiest struggle America had ever known… until now. "God help us," Darren prays softly.

And just then a large area of the town below goes dark.

The grid is going down. In his mind he hears that gigantic switch being flipped. Clank, clank. Two more sections are blackened. The entire scene is now void of light.

Deidra arrived safely in D.C. and quickly contacted her supervisor, reporting to work the next day, before power was lost in the capitol. She was sitting in the boss's office when the lights blinked several times. At quitting time an in-office memorandum was sent to everyone's desk suggesting that they stay put. The building had temporary power, and an old bunker below was still equipped with cots, food rations, water, and other necessities that could be used that night. Because she was not yet settled into her new apartment, Deidra decided to stay. It seemed to be what her new employer preferred, and she was determined to impress. About twenty percent of the workforce opted to do so.

An uneasy feeling told her that the tragedy of the quakes had not yet run its full course. Secretly, she wondered what information was being withheld from the public. With each passing hour she was becoming better informed and more aware of the magnitude of the disaster. Her sense was that government officials were scrambling, but chaos prevailed.

The Federal Emergency Management Agency, FEMA, was swamped. A tsunami might as well have hit the city, destroying the seat of the federal government, as the cries for help, calls for aid and assistance, were greater than a hurricane's force: a plea unfathomable, a need unmanageable, a challenge insurmountable.

There were rumors that other federal employees would be reassigned to assist with disaster relief efforts, and it was whispered among colleagues that the DNC should volunteer to join their ranks.

Everyone was waiting on pins and needles, longing to understand what had just happened, and what would next occur. The optimist offered words of reassurance, saying the power would most certainly be restored before morning. The pessimist warned of a doomsday scenario with apocalyptic impacts.

But in her self-made fantasy of confident assurance, Deidra could not even imagine the trouble that was coming her way.

Civil unrest was the bomb exploding everywhere in the crippled nation. Pandemonium teased the masses at first, but then gained a foothold as law and order faded away like the daylight at dusk on an overcast day, ushering in the midnight nightmare of sheer panic.

April 5:

It is the fifth day of the disaster.

Charlie, Ethel and their kids are barely managing in their futile attempt at operating a provisional shelter, but they are still healthy, the first and primary goal of survival. He is looking for a way to get more food, but a supply chain is nonexistent. The municipal water has stopped flowing. Heating appliances coughed and went out as their pilot lights were extinguished due to an interruption of natural gas.

They are wearing extra clothes, and sleep at night huddled together in the same room, on an extra mattress that was dragged there, into the master bedroom. The shotgun leans against the headboard near Charlie's place of unsettled rest. It is fully loaded, first with two blanks, then two rounds of rock salt, and finally with two shells filled with buckshot. He can advance to the lethal rounds very quickly using the gun's pump action.

With the dawn of each new day, their anxiety increases. If the sun is shining, they step outside to soak in the warmth of its rays, meager as it is.

There is a sump pump in the corner room of the basement where utilities are located. This small space has two doors, one interior and one exterior. The interior door opens to a finished family room. The other doorway is in the basement wall and leads to the outside backyard, with the cellar steps secured at ground level by steel doors. Charlie has removed the pump so that water can be bailed from its pit with a two-gallon bucket. The murky water is carried upstairs to the powder room where it is poured into the top of the toilet's tank. Its lid is perched precariously on the floor, leaning against the wall.

Water is being drained from the valve at the base of the fifty gallon tank heater. This they use for drinking, and as their leader, Charlie is beginning to ration it. They have not bathed since that fateful day, April fool's day, but if this is a prank of nature, or God, it is now overstated and totally unappreciated. Their plight is becoming serious.

They have been listening to their portable radio, but broadcasts are inconsistent, broken up, and often trail off, failing completely. During afternoon hours Charlie meets with his neighbors, on the street. They compare notes and share information they have gleaned from various sources. Rumors are rampant. He passes on to his family only encouraging news, after spinning it to be so, to the best of his ability, but then is seen whispering to Ethel as he reveals the unnerving truth of their plight.

Mr. Whittaker's son recently arrived back home from St. Louis. Whittaker is their neighbor, two houses down. The young man was lucky to get out of the city and even luckier to complete the trip. The highway is clogged with abandoned cars, many smashed, some in accidents and others damaged by vandals. Using back roads, detour after detour, and even a farmer's field, he maneuvered around the many blockades.

An angry mob is rioting in the city. At first they targeted malls and shopping centers, then smaller mom and pop stores, and now they are breaking into homes, raiding the affluent sections first. Dead bodies are lying in the street and the stench of dried blood in the gutters is attracting an enormous swarm of flies. Vermin are breeding everywhere.

Charlie grimaced at the thought. He had been thinking about leaving town in search of more food, but now is convinced to stay put. He should save what gasoline remains in his car, in case they need to suddenly flee for safety. But right now, they are going to remain, hunkered down.

Whittaker asks how the Sworsens' food pantry is holding up and Charlie immediately becomes nervous. Now squeamish, he shifts on his feet and quickly decides to exaggerate his shortage.

"We're just about out," he says and gives the elderly man a vile look. "Don't know what we'll eat after tomorrow."

"How about you?" he probes, hoping to intimidate his nosey neighbor.

But Whittaker shakes his head and quickly changes the subject, complaining about the lack of prescription medication. His gout is beginning to flare up again.

Charlie can't hide his lack of concern for his neighbor's discomfort. They part, suspicious and somewhat angry with each other; Whittaker limps slightly as he drags his left foot in the grass.

There are rumors of civil unrest in the larger cities nearby. Indianapolis has fallen into pandemonium. Angry mobs are moving into suburbia. Their attacks are ruthless. Their mentality is contagious.

Located five miles south of Bloomington and seven miles from Normal in a small rural town of 720 residents, Charlie is fearful of what his 80,000 neighbors to the north might be doing, or considering to do in this sorry state of affairs. Worse yet, he feels threatened by the two monsters rampaging as a single giant, a very serious threat that is too close for comfort: Indianapolis to the southeast and St. Louis to the southwest. Simply by clapping its hands together, this gargantuan can snatch the Sworsens. They are nothing more than a feeble bug, instantly crushed within its grasp.

April 9:

It is predawn and a noise arouses Charlie from his nightmare. It is the sound of glass being smashed.

He flies to the upstairs bedroom front window and in the dim light of morning sees a crowd of people on the street below.

Then, there is a loud banging on his front door. This disturbing sound reverberates through unoccupied rooms of his home announcing the threat of imminent intrusion.

Before stepping away from his vantage point on the second floor, he notices smoke billowing from another house nearby.

Everyone is awake now. His youngest, Alana, begins to cry.

"Charlie, you have to do something," Ethel warns with panic rising, as if he didn't already know of their predicament. But this is the moment he has prepared for, although reluctantly.

He pulls on the double-hung window, raising it two inches and places the barrel of his gun on its sill. Aiming toward the mob, he quickly fires his first shot. It is a blank, but still, it surprises them.

The smell of gunpowder permeates the stale air of their refuge. The banging has stopped, but just for a moment. He now hears them shouting with profanities and the noise downstairs resumes, with greater vigor. Some of the hoodlums are throwing rocks in return to his shot.

"Shawn, keep an eye on it. Everyone else, go in the bathroom and hide in the shower." Charlie pulls the gun from its firing port and steps quickly toward the hallway door. He pauses and looking back to his son further instructs, "Yell to me if they go to the back of the house."

From the landing on the stairs he can see that the front door is becoming loose on its hinges as a greater force is placed upon it by the intruders. He lifts his shotgun to aim once again, moving slowing forward.

Suddenly the door lurches and pops open. Charlie is standing face to face with an assailant. He fires a second shot, another blank. The young man stumbles backward and falls off the top step of the front stoop. The mob is pulling back.

Ka-chink. Charlie pumps the rifle to advance the next round.

Slowly his attacker rises, first looking to his chest in expectation of seeing torn flesh, a gaping and oozing wound. He begins to smile, an expression of gratification, an evil grin, and laughs hauntingly. He is still holding a sledge hammer in his right hand and lifts it to strike humanity with a fatal blow.

The third shot, rock salt, hits him squarely in the chest. The disheveled man wails like a dog when its tail is caught in the car door. He falls to the ground.

"Get the hell out of here or you will die!" Charlie yells vehemently and lets loose on the fourth round. Rock salt sprays into the mob that is staring at him like a bunch of zombies. They are already stunned by his attack on their leader. Their faces, arms, and legs burn instantly. Some are temporarily blinded, struck in their eyes. They begin to disperse, darting in all directions, like the horde of rats surprised by an alley cat as it pounces on them to retrieve their prize, scraps of food yanked from a torn garbage bag. The man at the door is crawling toward the other mobsters, stumbling forward in an urgent attempt to become erect from his hands and knees, now bleeding.

Their assault has been thwarted. Charlie kicks at the door to force it back into its jambs. He is trembling uncontrollably, overwhelmed with fear and consumed in the rush of adrenaline.

He runs up the stairs to check on his family. They are huddled together in the bathroom. He pulls them to himself, arms open wide, for a group hug. There is a spontaneous round of quick kisses, celebrating the realization of survival with a new appreciation for life.

Charlie reaches for the box of ammo. It is time to reload, and this time, he is arming himself with buckshot.

April 11:

Joseph has made his way to Joliet. Leaving carnage in his wake, he was determined not be deterred from his mission. The home for the aged is barricaded behind a line of abandoned delivery trucks. Two men armed with AR-15 assault rifles stand boldly on the rooftop, protecting their elderly parents and their families seeking refuge inside. Their emergency supply of food and water has been enough to sustain the majority of the inhabitants, although the temporary morgue is filled to capacity.

Barbara's reluctant decision to relinquish her wellbeing to institutional care has proven to be a wise one. Although in a weakened state, she has survived the bedlam.

"State your name and your purpose," a man commands from his perch above. Their guns are pointed at Joseph.

"Joseph Daniels. I'm looking for my mother. Barbara Daniels."

Another armed man appears from behind the center truck. "Show me your ID," he demands. "But first, if you're carrying, drop your gun right there on the ground."

Joseph points to the indicated spot, intending to cause a distraction.

"That's right. Put it there, right in front of where you're standing."

Joseph tosses a pistol toward the man but keeps the small revolver that is tucked in his waistband at the small of his back.

"Okay now, put your hands in the air, nice and high, where I can see them."

Joseph is not a man accustomed to surrender. Gritting his teeth, he focuses for resolve and self control. He knows that he must carefully choose his battles but prefers to accept the challenge of the opposition in this unpleasant confrontation. He's feeling the strong desire to engage the enemy once again. He is confident that he can overpower them.

Soon he is escorted by a tall, thin man into a dark room. An elderly woman is lying there in her bed. Alongside her, on top of the blanket is a wooden box. It appears that it could be a music box, but it is longer than such a collectible usually is. Joseph suspects that it may be a jewelry box, although it is very plain. He has never seen it before. It is made of walnut with dovetailed corners, the meticulous work of a craftsman. There are no hinges or latches on the box.

A chill penetrates the air heavy with the smell of dried urine.

"We tried to get her to move into the main compound, but she refused," the man offered in defense of the deplorable situation she had obviously endured. Many questions were racing through his brain, but Joseph decided not to pursue them at this time.

"I'll give you a minute," the man suggested in a monotone, and turned to leave, as if he was attending the parlor of a funeral home, offering a son the privacy needed to gather his thoughts to say goodbye to his mother. No doubt, this was a role he had served many times before.

This reunion was nothing like the one Joseph had imagined many times before, while resting in the barracks, lying on his cot, wide awake in the middle of the night. He expected to be sitting at his usual place at the dining room table, its right side, against the wall, around the corner from his father who resided as the head of the household. In his vision, Fred is smiling, happy to be reunited with his long lost son. He is listening intently as Joseph describes a tour of duty and beams at the news of his son, heroic on the battlefield, awarded the Silver Star for gallantry in action. His father proclaims, "You should have received the Medal of Honor!"

His mother is in the kitchen pulling a homemade apple pie out of the oven. It is Joseph's favorite dessert. She is strong, capable as always, and still feisty, even as she listens intently to the words drifting in from the adjoining room.

Barbara was woman that always exhibited the posture of nobility. She had dark brown hair, and the clothes and accessories with which she adorned herself presented an orderly appearance that was impeccable.

Joseph brought a chair from the corner of the room and placed it alongside her bed. He watched with wonder and waited for her to stir.

Fifteen minutes and a thousand questions amended with regret ten times greater than their unknowing, pressed upon him. Her breathing was shallow. Her hair was white. As he looked at her wrinkled and blotched skin, he saw an eye twitch.

His heart was heavy as he felt the burdens of her life, still largely unknown to him, but now fully on display, highlighted by the deep ravines that cut through her cheeks, drawn as they are. They remind him of the ditches in the desert wasteland, formed by brutal storms and flash floods. Water, the essence of life, was so lacking and badly needed there, yet, when it did finally arrive, it came with madness, a swift current, and quickly ran away from the thirsty sponge of earth still devoid of life. The rain of promise did not stay to sustain the land, victim of a broken relationship.

He reached for her hand and held it gently. It was cold and limp, like the wet leaf that falls from its branch on a frosty autumn morning after a heavy rainfall the day before.

She stirred.

"Mother?" he inquired softly.

She turned her head toward him and slowly opened her eyes. Her eyelids were heavy; her eyes blurry and bloodshot. Thick yellow mucus resided there, a curtain against light, a lure unto the void of death.

She looked intently, without any movement. Her eyes brightened some and she blurted, "Fred?" and blinked, "Is it you?"

Joseph grimaced.

"No, Ma, it's me… Joseph," he sighed.

She was staring now, eyes wide in confusion.

"No, it can't be," her mind wandered, becoming irrational. She was stunned by the proclamation, "he is dead," and she looked away. "It was a long time ago," she nearly whispered.

"Mother, I have come back for you."

And there was a long pause as no one spoke in that moment, even as Joseph waited to be validated.

Barbara began to turn her head toward her son once again but stopped midway and replied in a soft growl, "Fred said you're a coward," and she completed the turn to make eye contact. Her eyes locked onto his.

That missile of condemnation penetrated even to his heart as it exploded in his brain. For many years he had been absent as the battles of the home front raged on, without any assistance or contribution from this prodigal son. Their lives hadn't remained paused after his disappearance. Theirs' was a loss too great to calculate, its effect unknown. Perhaps Fred would not have fallen off that slippery roof that fateful morning, if he had had the assistance of his capable son, working alongside him. But the considerations of *perhaps* and *what if* had long since been forgotten, far from reality. Thirty-five long, very long years, had separated them. The son of promise did not stay to sustain the family, victim of a broken relationship.

Joseph stiffened and retrieved his hand as he straightened his back. He looked away, and his mother watched him closely.

"Ma... I went to fight another war," he said with regret. "I am sorry, truly sorry, for any hardship I caused you."

Silence – a moment of time that seemed like an eternity.

"Joey, I'm glad to see you," she grinned slightly and reached for him.

"We're getting out of here," Joseph said, assuming command once again.

He scoops her up and his mother leans her head against his chest, listening to his strong heart as it beats with the pulse of love long lost, but now revived, carrying her in his arms, nestled there like a cherished bride as she is hoisted over the threshold of the newlyweds' nest, ushering in their new life together. And this elderly woman is holding a wooden box, the one item too important to leave behind, the treasure that has been precious to the Daniels for many generations.

April 17:

Gassed out of their bunkers like moles in a burrow, the President and his cabinet are captured and incarcerated along with the majority of the members of Congress. Sections of the capitol building have been demolished by the terrorists' rocket propelled grenades, RPG's.

Outside of the major cities, except for those in the state of California, most people have survived, but barely, as huge numbers of people are in dire need of medical attention.

Smoldering are its remains, a broken pile of scorched wooden rubble, the former Coronado hotel. It had entertained prominent people for nearly 150 years as a world class tourist resort. It was a Victorian palace, a historical marvel located near the once proud city of San Diego.

But all that glory is gone now. The Golden State lies in ruins. It was a maddening place even before it was struck by North Korean bombs shortly after the earthquake. Now it is a war zone, littered with hundreds of thousands of causalities, the terminal events both natural and manmade.

April 19:

Darren is wondering why he has not heard from his supervising commander. He used the Military Auxiliary Radio System, MARS, to message his Sergeant during the previous night. It is rumored that Olympus, code for the White House, has fallen. He commands his Jeep to push against gravity as he races up the mountain, anxious to arrive at his station in the command center.

Deidra sat in her recliner all night long, thinking about and anticipating her next move. It is now obvious that the republic and its two major parties are forever gone. There will no longer be Republicans, and this, she thinks, is a good thing. But the Democratic Party has also disbanded during the shutdown and incarceration of the federal government.

"So it's gone," she affirms herself. *"What's next?"* she ponders. And then the thought occurs to her that she should quickly pledge her loyalty to the new occupying Muslim force. This will place her ahead of others who will seek office with them, making her more likely to rise in the new hierarchy of power. She urgently desires this advantage.

Is she willing to abandon American patriotism and Christian faith, the foundations of her upbringing? *"Oh yes!"* She thinks that this is her best chance for advancement in the new world order. *"The possibilities are endless!"* the shouting idea echoes within her brain arousing a feeling of delight.

With confidence in herself, she plans her next move. She has no desire to remain dormant in want of days gone by, the pitiful place of regret. *"The past is the past."* She despises "good ol' days."

Deidra knows that there are pockets of resistance that continue to fight, located mainly in the less populated middle to western states of the north, places in the Dakotas, Wyoming, Montana, Idaho, and others. And she is confident that the insurgency will soon be contained.

She doesn't care if her twin brother is one of those imprisoned. The poor choices he made, the course of his life unto doom, cannot and will not be her burden. *"How could he have been so stupid?"*

And with her condemnation Darren suddenly feels a stab at his heart and the presence of evil in his midst.

Hell's Revenge: Self Sufficiency is a Brigadier General in Satan's army. His goal is to make a soul callous, hardened by the mind's ascertained position that she, or he, does not need God, with an absolute determination to continually disregard the Savior's plea. This demon has now accomplished his work in Deidra's heart. She is totally uncaring toward the plight of others, blinded by selfish ambition, and consumed with pride.

Self Sufficiency is now ready to file a report with his ranking officer, Rebellion. If this next General in the line of command can inflame Deidra with his poison, rebellion toward God in active opposition to Christ, or in a grave passivity of leisure indulgence that locks the conscience in death's grasp so that it cannot be stirred, the resurrection of her spirit unto true life is most unlikely.

Heaven's Repose: The Creator has ordained free will for all human beings and His holy law cannot be usurped. Still, the Savior desires that no one should be lost, and grieves for an overtly determined young woman who has listened to and obeyed the persuasion of evil. Jesus knocks persistently at her heart's door, pleading to sup with her. The Spirit instructs godly relatives to plant seeds of truth, but the soil of Deidra's heart is as broken rocks crowded by thorns and thistles.

The precious and innocent Lamb that was slain for the sins of the world has been found to be worthy of opening the seals of the book of revelation unto God's final judgments.

There is much to be done in the spiritual realm at this time, as the age of grace draws to a predetermined end. It is all in accordance with His plan. The Prince of Peace rallies in joy at the knowing of His imminent return.

He is also desirous to engage in hand-to-hand combat with Satan. He longs for this devil's capture and the end of his reign of tyranny. It will happen soon, but first, that lying Beast will attempt to entice all of humanity.

And the seventh seal yet remains, sealed still.

Darren walks briskly as he enters the GCS . The guard usually posted at the front gate is strangely missing today. No one stands near the sign that boldly identifies the facility with the letters, "ΛHΛB". The gate is already hoisted in the open position. Doors normally secured are swinging freely or hanging open. Pieces of paper, pages of stray documents, litter the floor in the hallways.

Inside the large room that contains individual offices, there is a flurry of unorganized activity. Darren approaches his cubicle and pauses to speak with Rosalyn, the airman first class who occupies the space next to his. She is grabbing at folders in a file drawer.

"Hey Roz, what's doing?" he prods.

With eyebrows raised she gives him a look of contempt.

Darren leans on the office divider and watches her, hoping to be noticed. He sees a paper she has dropped and quickly bends to pick it up. Holding it out to her, their eyes meet.

"You don't know?" she asks, finally acknowledging his advance.

Darren simply shakes his head indicating a negative response.

"You really don't know?" she persists. "Come on!"

"What?!" he finally speaks again with an urgent request for information.

Rosalyn sighs and tosses a folder onto a pile on her desktop.

"We're done. Dismissed!" and she catches his look of disbelief. "Yes sir, discharged! No papers. No pay, no bennies," and she pauses to watch for his response.

"You're kidding me... Right?"

"No sir, it's over," she replies firmly. A short statement purposed for terminating his career.

Darren sits in his desk chair and leans back, staring at his computer monitor.

"Wipe it. Erase the memory, or yank out the hard drive. Make it clean, or they will have even more evidence against you," she instructs with urgency.

"You've got to be kidding me," he persists in repetition as he expresses his disbelief.

"Darren!" she commands with aggitation, "They are coming. Get out while you can. Leave nothing behind with your name on it." And then Roz returns to her task with increased vigor.

"Nice knowing you, buddy," she offers in reconciliation. "I hope you have a good life," she says while looking at her screen and tapping on the keyboard. "You're a good guy."

Shortly after that day of infamy, April 17, the day when members of the executive and legislative branches of the government of the United States of America were captured, the grid was restored. Civility is ordered in Washington D.C. and a Muslim militia fans out to reclaim other metropolitan areas.

April 22:

Two days ago, Darren received a message from his grandmother urging him to meet with her in Michigan. She provided an address unfamiliar to him and included its GPS coordinates, which he thought was strange. It was the last text message to appear on his phone before he smashed it with a hammer. He was happy to learn that his grandmother was still alive.

But still, he wondered why he had not been contacted by his sister. He remembered her affectionate hug in Bloomington after they shared that intimate breakfast. But he has no way of reaching her.

He has been busy during the past 72 hours: packing, concealing, and burning documents

As good fortune would have it, he discovered a corpse in an abandoned car along Route 52 in a remote area of West Virginia. He gagged at its intense smell. Holding a handkerchief over his mouth and nose, he quickly reached into the man's rear pocket for his wallet. The deceased was about his size and although probably fifteen years older, he was close enough in appearance to become a substitute.

Darren took his driver's license and put his own in its place, returned the wallet, and then exchanged license plates on the cars. He twisted some newspaper into a rope and fished it into the gas tank's filler hose. He lighted it and then waited at a distance. The fire was effective for accomplishing his purpose.

Darren has assumed a new identity. He is already sporting the beginnings of a thick beard, similar to that of the deceased stranger.

May 10:

Someone is pounding on Charlie's front door. He peers out from his upstairs vantage point and sees a Humvee parked on his lawn. A man is standing in his yard, looking in his direction. He knows that Charlie is inside.

Reluctantly, Charlie opens the door, but just a crack.

"Mr. Sworsen?" an Arab man inquires in a heavy accent. "Are you here?"

"No! He's not here," Charlie lies in reply, "Killed in the riots."

"Mr. Sworsen, I think you are he," he exclaims in return and forcefully pushes against the door, thrusting it fully open. He has drawn his service revolver and is pointing it directly at Charlie.

"You now have two choices," he instructs in monotone. "Give me your firearms, or come with me now!" he demands. He looks back to his comrade and inquires, "What does he have?"

"A 12 gauge shotgun," the other man in civilian clothes replies firmly. He appears to be American.

"Sworsen, give me the rifle," he redirects.

"It's upstairs," Charlie admits reluctantly. "I... I... I've got to go upstairs to get it," he stammers.

"You have two minutes to relinquish your weapon to me," the uniformed man replies while looking at his clipboard. He waves his revolver toward the steps. "Go! Get it now!"

Charlie turns to see his son Shawn and daughter Larissa watching from the landing above, peering over the banister. Ethel is standing there in the silence, holding their daughter's hand.

Chapter 6

The ultimate imprisonment of the soul is found in rebellion against God. It can be expressed in multiple ways, and common are defiance, or its opposite, which is passivity.

Traffic is light on Interstate 75 as Darren comes near to Toledo. He decides to stop at a large truck stop in hopes of finding the provisions necessary for continuing his road trip. He needs fuel and food.

Duct tape was used to attach a large piece of cardboard in place over a smashed window on the front of the building. Only one gas pump was working, the hose handles of the others covered with plastic shopping sacks. His is the only car parked at the front of the store.

The warm sunshine of spring heralds for new life to sprout forth, but somehow the gloom of tragedy prevails upon its call. Even the birds, usually singing in proclamation with a joyful refrain, are strangely silent and scarce in this place.

Inside the shelves are mostly bare, a few cupcakes and bags of pretzels, a brand he doesn't recognize, occupy the top shelf. Their price has quadrupled, as indicated by the hand written sign there. As Darren approaches the counter he sees a middle aged man of Arabian descent, sporting a long, unkempt beard. His eyes are thin, behind narrow glasses and dark lenses. On the window sill behind him a handgun is prominently displayed, an obvious deterrent for shoplifters and looters.

Another handwritten sign on the back of the cash register says, "Cash Dollars Only." Darren completes his purchase quickly without speaking a word to the clerk who is also serving as guard. Even this simple transaction feels threatening.

Relieved to be getting back on the road, he approaches the on ramp, and stops quickly after observing a caravan coming toward him. The approaching vehicles have their headlights on, and a sheriff's car is in front with blinking strobe lights. Darren pulls off, onto the shoulder of the ramp, before getting any closer to the highway. He doesn't want to attract their attention.

They are black cars with tinted windows, typical of government issue for official business. He sees Cadillacs and Suburbans, the first with small flags attached to the front fenders. There are four, five, six, seven vehicles that race past, with a M1026 Humvee at the end of the line. It has a MK19 grenade launcher and a M2 machine gun mounted on top.

Not stars and stripes, no red, white and blue, the banner they display is green and white. It has the symbol of the jihadist revolution, a crescent moon and star with Arabic writing.

Sheikhs of the new regime are enroute to the Islamic Center of America, located in Dearborn, Michigan. It is to be a center for regional government under the Ulema.

The Islamic Center of Washington D.C. is being expanded and renovated to serve as a palace, a place of residence for the Monarch. Leaders of the new Islamic nation have already announced plans to revamp the monuments of the city. The capitol building will become a great mosque and qubba. The peninsula, host of the East Potomac Park, will ideally serve as a sahn, a large courtyard which will accommodate the masses of pilgrims who will come for prayer. With renovation the Washington Monument will be transformed into a minaret and will announce the call to prayer. The Jefferson Memorial is to be converted to serve as a mihrab, indicating the direction of Mecca, the qibla. The Lincoln Memorial will be used as a jama masjid, a congregational mosque for Friday prayers for high ranking officials.

Construction of this great shrine of Islam is already underway.

Darren's route is north toward the Huron National Forest and hours later he passes through the woodlands of the Atlanta State Forest. He turns onto a dirt road and after tolerating many miles of ruts, washboard, large holes filled with mud, and narrow bridges, he suddenly stomps on the brakes. There, to his left is a narrow lane that leads into the woods under the low hanging limbs of a Hemlock tree. It appears as though a vehicle has passed through here recently. Tire tracks and ruts are well formed.

He enters and parks a distance from the old mobile home now visible from this advanced vantage point. There are no cars here, but tracks continue around one end of the trailer. There is a single light inside. A shadow crosses over the small window.

It feels like a trap. Darren thinks about his grandmother and is flooded with emotion. Melancholy. It hits him like a tidal wave.

The sun is setting rapidly and shadows stretch over the small clearing, striking upon the hood of his car. The light inside the trailer appears to be brighter now, and as a beacon it summons him.

Darren is road weary and feels lost in this forest. Perhaps he should just lean back, fall asleep, and like Rip Van Winkle wake up decades later. Things would surely be better then, or would they?

Words from a lecture he attended during basic training resonate in his mind. "The remedy for melancholy is a passion to serve justice." This was said to be the motivation of the great president, Abraham Lincoln, during the war of all wars. It was the greatest struggle America ever endured, that is, until now.

"Justice for all," – it is merely a shadow, a lofty principle from the statues of freedom this land once knew.

"…it stands, one Nation under God, indivisible, with liberty and justice for all." It was the Pledge of Allegiance of that great Republic.

But that is now history. The memory of it is as a shadow cast upon a country defeated, as its star fades and is about to be completely extinguished.

He reaches for his gun. This he can grasp; the shadow, he cannot. Hope is fleeting. But inside, there is still an ember. It barely glows. After all, he is a soldier. He must keep fighting and die believing, all the while chasing the shadows.

Darren opens his car door.

Inside the dingy hunting cabin, under dim light, Barbara drops a plate in front of Joseph. Dinner has been served: warmed raviolis from a can with a slice of stale bread and butter.

"Did you hear that?" he asks and jumps up. Barbara's eyes are wide with sudden fright.

Joseph pulls back a curtain and looks out, through the fogged glass. "Someone's here. Get my gun," he orders precisely.

Barbara doesn't reach for the weapon, but moves to the next window, and peers out.

"Relax. It's Darren," she announces. "He did come," she continues. "I knew he would."

She seems spry as she skips to the door and pulls hard against the handle. It sticks.

"Darren, I knew you'd come," she exclaims, with arms wide open for a hug as she looks longingly into the face of her grandson.

Letting go of the revolver in his pants pocket, Darren reaches for her embrace, while stepping inside.

"Oh, you're a sight for sore eyes." And she hugs him again. "Let me see you." She reaches with both hands to cradle his chin. "Oh my, you're as handsome as ever."

"Gram, what are you doing here?" he asks urgently. "How did you ever find this place?" He assumes that she has been hiding here since the quake.

"Oh, this old place?" she concedes. "Your grandfather brought me here once," she remembers, "but that was a very long time ago."

Darren waited for more information, some that would make sense.

"You know," she paused, "he liked to hunt for deer." And she reminded, "I thought he brought you and Deidra here once."

"No, not here," Darren replied slowly. Then he saw the figure of a man standing behind the wall divider, near the kitchen sink. He instinctively reached for his weapon and asked, "Who is that!?"

It was an awkward moment made by thirty years of absence, and confusion quickly came upon her. "Joseph!" she proclaimed. "Ethel's little brother."

"What? It can't be," Darren responded as he looked to his grandmother for clarification. Secretly, he wondered if she was beginning to be senile.

The strange man took a step toward them.

Darren felt for the gun's grip.

"Aunt Ethel's brother?" he whined, still not making the

connection.

"Yes," Barbara finally found clarity of thought. "Darren… this is

your father!"

The young man gasped and recoiled with a backwards step as the

elder man approached with an extended hand.

"I often saw the MQ-1 Predator do a low flyby," he suggested,

hoping for common ground. "It was an honor to have served with you."

Joseph smiled and held his outstretched open hand steady. His heart

pounded in his chest. He had a son. This was his new reality.

Darren accepted the ghostly gesture and felt his hand squeezed

by rough skin, real flesh and blood. This was no apparition. This was

now reality for him, too.

Three days went quickly by as three needy souls lived in

seclusion, recluse and caring little about the troubles of the nation or the

world. During this lapse of time and reality, a father and son began the

journey of becoming acquainted, the very first step of forming a

connection, and then, much more than that, the enduring relationship they both desired. Each had a multitude of questions but showed restraint, waiting for the appropriate time to delve deeper into the other's psyche. They first shared their military service record, and then told war stories. Darren was quickly disarmed by this man's calm resolve, the eminence of his capable and commanding stature.

"So you were the pilot of those UAV's?" (Unmanned Aerial Vehicles), Joseph asked.

"Yeah," Darren answered informally. "They put me in a new program with their fastest aircraft," he offered. "Guess I was doing pretty good."

"What were those small ones?" Joseph pictured the desert in his mind. "We called them Blackbirds. They'd chase after cars, and wow, they delivered a big punch. They looked like mini Stealths."

"I loved flying them!"Darren exclaimed. "It was the Peregrine CIM (Combative In Motion) aircraft. I could turn it just by leaning in my chair. Its speed topped out at 480 KPM. They were weaponized with a miniaturized nuke."

Joseph had removed his cap and was scratching his head.

"The miniaturized missile allowed them to develop a much smaller, faster, more agile aircraft," Darren explained. "Yeah, they are way cool. Combative in motion: what a concept in hi-tech."

Barbara became almost invisible to the duo, but listened intently in a glimmering of pride. She was thinking about her late husband, his late father, the younger's late grandfather. Fred would have been joyful in this moment. And then she thought about life's lesson. This reunion was something unexpected. Never could she have imagined it; at this unusual time, in this strange place, in this most dramatic way. So Barbara, an elderly woman, in her own right deserving of self pity and the wallowing of depression, decided at that moment not to give up on life, but to live with an expectation of something good, even though she couldn't imagine what might happen next. Fred would have wanted her to live this way.

She thought about her godly man, her partner in life. She envisioned him dwelling with the Most High, and smiling in his heavenly abode. The Creator of such things surely must be good, she concluded, and her faith in God caused hope to blossom within her soul. It brought new life, the first true sign of Spring.

It was the fourth day, after a light breakfast of toast and cereal, that Joseph offered, "Darren, I have something to show you." He went down the hallway into a bedroom and returned with a small wooden box in his hands. He placed it on the table in front of this son and slowly slid the lid off one end to open it and expose its contents.

Darren looked intently and saw an envelope inside.

"Go ahead," his father urged. "This is the family treasure your grandfather told you about."

He gulped and looked again at the box. He gently lifted out an envelope, torn across one end. It was addressed in longhand, the cursive letters neat and well formed. The letter had been sent to "Mr. Levi Daniels, 1050 Molly Pitcher Highway, Greencastle, Pennsylvania." There was no postage stamp, but in its place, in the top, right corner were hand written letters: "A. Lincoln."

Darren held the centuries old envelope lightly, and turned it over for examination. The torn edges at the other end were faded and brittle. The envelope was mostly white but had dark blotches.

"Really?" he asked. "Abraham Lincoln?" he nearly stuttered, "a letter from President Lincoln?"

"Yes, that's right," Joseph answered with reverence. "Your ancestor, Levi Daniels, and the late great President, were well acquainted before Lincoln was elected," he explained, "while he was a lawyer."

"Wow, this is awesome," Darren exclaimed softly, mimicking his father's reverent expression. He paused in wonder. "What does it say?"

Joseph nodded in permission. "Go ahead," he repeated. "This is a message travelled through time, meant just for us."

Darren puzzled.

He pulled a paper from the envelope at the end that was ripped off by its anxious receiver, a grandfather called Levi. Darren could not know what that man felt at that time, but the excitement continued until this day, his time to participate in a personal and private conversation with a legend, Abraham Lincoln, the 16th President of the United States.

The letter was tri-folded and Darren opened it gently, not putting pressure on the creases. The paper was thick, with the feel of linen. Its edges were worn and exhibited small tears. Fibers in the pulped cloth were bleached. In age, the paper had yellowed and become brittle.

Letters printed on the top of the page with the use of a bold gothic typestyle proclaimed, "Executive Mansion." On the second line was printed one word, "Washington." The date was indicated with the first three digits of the year pre-printed, "186" and completed with the addition of the final digit, handwritten. It was the number "3". "1863." In front of the year the date was completed by the author's hand, "April 1,".

Darren cleared his throat and began to read aloud:

"To my Dear Friend Levi:"

He paused and smiled at his father, then continued.

"Cheers to our former shared affiliation, the great Whigs! The time spent in those sometimes tumultuous debates has served me well. I hope this letter finds you and yours in good health and with prosperity."

"This war weighs heavy upon my heart. The loss is great and many days I feel a great responsibility for it from whence comes a greater determination for victory. Our righteous soldiers, great patriots of the Republic, shall not have suffered and died in vain! We shall persevere. God have mercy."

"If I had had my way, this war would never have been commenced. It would have been ended before this, if I had been allowed my way, but we find it still continues."

"Our cause is worthy and ordained. Our victory will be great for all mankind. Thusly, we must endure. The Republic must be saved!"

"Some have claimed that we fight for God in a holy war for Righteousness. I am not so emboldened to speak in representation of the Almighty, but have the faith to believe that God requires our unrelenting faithfulness and endurance in these difficult times. Surely He intends some great good to follow which no mortal could make, or stay. Do not fall into doubt and despair during this mighty convulsion. We must believe in Divine Providence; the will of Almighty God in this struggle, and live in humble obedience. In this life we prepare for the next: eternal."

"Fervently do I pray - that this mighty scourge of war speedily pass away. May the sacrifice of so many generate a new hope abounding in grace, with a helping hand extended one to another in peace forgiving, the fruit of true repentance. Surely this I know, that Almighty God is not mocked. He will accept the sacrifice of the forthright and many have paid the ultimate price for these benefits of freedom."

"America must and will endure. We are a mighty nation, His favored land, founded on the principles of Christianity."

"I pray that you and your family will find safe refuge in passage of this great travail. But be forewarned, the army of the Confederacy is advancing northward by way of Pennsylvania. Take necessary precautions for continued survival."

"God help us all."

"Yours truly,

A Lincoln"

Darren exhaled a long sigh that whistled softly between his lips. "We have to share this," he announced, suddenly swelling with pride and inspiration. "With America," and he sighed again less exuberantly, "what's left of her." He wiped a tear that was forming at the corner of his right eye.

"But how?" Joseph and Barbara spoke in unison and then smiled approvingly at each other.

"A burner phone," Darren was thinking out loud. "And YouTube," he scratched the back of his head. "I think I can post a video with a burner phone."

The other two looked on with puzzled amazement.

"I'll have to go into town tomorrow," Darren suggested, "to get what I need," he concluded. "I need to find one with a video camera."

Deidra is being escorted into what was the Pentagon, now the headquarters of the regime for the UISA, United Islamic States of America. She has an appointment with the Caliphate, as she is being considered for a position with the Intermediary. Essentially a press secretary or assistant in public relations, this person works with the Minister of Information, and is charged with convincing others of a former persuasion unto full cooperation with the UISA.

If selected, her job will be to defend and advance their propaganda.

But her presence is a contradiction of the influence they seek to administer over residents of the fallen nation. Secretly, Deidra has rebelled against all religious authority.

She was told to dress appropriately, and walks with a prideful swagger, an expression of the defiance she cannot entirely squelch. Wearing the traditional abayas and hijab, she experiences restricted movement. The covering is uncomfortable and she feels her head beginning to sweat.

Underneath the gown she wears modern clothes symbolic of the western culture she still lusts for. This she does in defiance; with loyalty to the true liberation she remains committed to, the cause of freedom for all women in the world.

They cannot see what is underneath or know what is inside. She is purposed only for personal advancement. She will play their game, but holds closer in her heart the principle of privilege for all women.

A man walks with short, brisk steps and passes without turning his head, refusing to acknowledge the women passing in single file on the opposite side of the hallway. He wears a white thobe enhanced with a red and white checkered keffiyeh. Secretly, Deidra prefers his fashion accessory and wonders how a tryst with him might transpire.

She is placed in a small room in front of a desk. At its one end there is a camera mounted on a tripod. Another Muslim woman enters moments later and begins speaking in an Arabic dialect. Deidra responds with, "English, please."

Her instructor continues with a heavy Middle Eastern accent and tells Deidra to look directly into the camera and recite the pledge.

Deidra has memorized it the night before. With eyes cold as ice and a tone tough as steel she lifts her chin and boldly proclaims:

"As an American Muslim, I pledge allegiance to Allah and His Prophet. I respect and love my family and my community and I dedicate my life to serving this cause. As an American citizen, with rights and responsibilities, I pledge allegiance to the flag of the United Islamic States of America, and to the Sharia for which it stands, one Ummah, with truth and justice for all."

She nods and smiles modestly with her lips pursed. *"Yeah, right,"* she silently reaffirms herself with mental sarcasm.

Next she is handed a document that requires her signature, witnessed by the cohort of Islamic domination. It explicitly states that Jesus is a false prophet and that his resurrection is a false claim. Deidra is not bothered by the blasphemy of Christianity. She quickly signs the confession and hands it back with a grin.

Hell's Revenge: Rebellion has achieved his ultimate goal. Evil has fortified its presence upon her soul. Deidra is at the precipice of a great fall, even demonic possession. She will now be directed to take further action in denial of the Sovereign, and urged to receive the mark, the designation of loyalty to Satan. Her doom has been firmly established in evil's foundation of deception and lies.

Heaven's Repose: The souls of martyred saints cry for retribution. They have been clothed in pure white gowns and dressed for the wedding feast of the Lamb. They need but rest a little longer, as the time of their reward draws nigh.

The Messiah sends his angels to testify once again for the encouragement and preservation of the saints. His banquet table is prepared.

Darren's video is trending, spreading like wildfire on the internet. Essentially, it is a call to arms and perseverance for the remaining rebels, insurgent fighters for America, true and unyielding patriots. Their mantra has become, "Freedom Never Dies. We Will Endure," and Lincoln's own words, credited to him, "The Republic Must Be Saved!" There are rumors of new uprisings with government munitions captured in a raid led by inspired Texans.

The recorded message shows Joseph reading the Lincoln letter, introduced as a family heirloom recently discovered, and Darren with a battle cry while brandishing an AR-15 assault rifle. Their faces are unashamedly exposed although their names are withheld.

Darren hoped this would prove the statements of his commanding officer to be true. During training it was stated, "Today, revolutions are fueled by postings on YouTube." Another quote that influenced Darren's reasoning was, "Never tell a soldier that he does not understand the cost of war." Darren knew that many hearing his call to arms had already been close to another who paid the ultimate price and that they were inspired by the sacrifice. Once that experience was revisited with Lincoln's provocation, the soldier would have reaffirmed purpose and renewed determination.

During his last trip into Hillman for supplies he was made to feel uncomfortable by their glances, double takes and stares from strangers, and for awhile Darren suspected that he was being followed. He told his father about his concerns and Joseph did not hesitate in stating, "We have to get out of here… keep moving."

Darren looked unsure. "What about Gram?" he asked.

"She is safer without us," Joseph informed matter-of-factly. "We are now wanted men."

Darren nodded in dismay at the reality of this new threat. It is one they had anticipated, and would not by terrorized by.

"We leave, first thing in the morning. Daybreak. Start packing," he felt like a commanding officer once again.

"We'll take Mom to a safe place outside of Milwaukee," Joseph reasoned. "We'll get her a motel suite there," he concluded. "She should change her name – assume a new identity."

"Where do we go?" Darren asked with anticipation.

"Camping. We'll live off nature," his father answered. "How are your survival skills?"

Darren was dazed.

"We will disappear for a while, until we find a new unit to join with," his new commanding officer concluded.

Like Lincoln as he considered the threat of assassination, the peril they faced was feigned and exaggerated as it was forced into submission unto the genetic trait they shared. In the face of martyrdom the shadow of their military past presented more than an elusive silhouette; it was the alchemy of invisible reinforcement, extreme determination under duress.

Standing this morning at the railing of the ship's stern, Darren stiffens and raises his collar to deflect the moist, cold air. His shivering upon the ferry that races across Lake Michigan is more than a rejection of the wind's chill, it is releasing the great magnitude of tension he has stored within: stress caused by the series of recent and traumatic events in his life. But at this moment he has found respite, an escape from his feelings of doubt, uncertainty, remorse, and yes, even fear.

The sun is shining upon the water, painting a pathway of shimmering light to its promise of life renewed. Ripples in the distance are crowned in white like jewels reflecting the light. The waves closer to the ferry boil in excitement, all the while bathing in the highlights provided by earth's star. Seagulls are squawking as they provide escort, as if they know the way. All seems as it should be. All seems to be harmonious.

Barbara is sitting in an inside lounge, sipping on a Styrofoam cup of hot coffee. She appears to be content in her moment of comfort.

Joseph has gone to the highest point on the ship's bow. Like the figurehead of a great sailing ship with three masts, he stares off toward their distant destination, not yet visible, believing that land will soon emerge and their mooring will offer success to their mission. He is stone faced with determination, an expression much like that which he exhibited on the battlefield. But obviously, Joseph is enjoying the contrast of this place, caught up in the beauty of the alluring scene.

Open air, wide spaces, nothing to encumber the freedom of the spirit– there is happiness for the heart here.

Joseph decided to take the Lake Express high speed ferry from Muskegon, Michigan, as they launched their journey to Milwaukee, Wisconsin. The eighty miles over open water on the world's fifth largest lake would take 150 minutes and erase 200 miles from their road trip, saving them approximately four hours of travel time.

Each one of the trio, in their own way, finds this time to be exhilarating, a recharge that is desperately needed for the challenges they are about to face. For now, they have escaped, but the waiting dock and discharge will put them back into the land of strife.

This lapse of time gives them a lull that allows them to have breathing space –the regeneration of not just their cells by a new and plentiful supply of oxygen, but an anchoring of their determination, as relief provides healing for the soul.

Joseph found a beautiful old Victorian house, a Bed and Breakfast, on what was once a distinguished Wisconsin estate, built during the eighteenth century by a local entrepreneur who made his fortune with the Milwaukee railroad. His grandson engineered and placed into service the "Hiawatha," a streamlined steamer that was considered to be hi-tech and high-speed. This was the former summer residence of Alexander Mitchell.

At first the place seemed to be abandoned, but after approaching the rear door sheltered by a large porch, a young woman with two toddlers in tow, hollered for her husband, and a contemporary appearing man opened it suspiciously. They had no guests, and weren't expecting any. Joseph introduced himself as a veteran of foreign wars, returned to the states to take care of his mother, and asked for a hearing of his plight.

He entered cautiously.

The owner of the house studied him with an obvious intensity. "I think I know you," he finally admitted. "The Lincoln letter. You're the guy on that video."

"Is that a good thing, or bad?" Joseph quickly inquired, his battle instincts aroused.

"Well I sure was impressed!" the man answered. "I'm Jason, and very pleased to make your acquaintance," he said, offering his hand in greeting. Joseph accepted his introduction with relief.

"You really rallied the troops," Jason confirmed. "I'd have joined up with them," he paused, "they're still in hiding until they get better organized."

"But I have my wife and daughters to look after," he explained, "she can't manage this place all by herself. We put in a big garden this year."

"Certainly, I understand," Joseph agreed.

"So where you headed?" the estate owner asked, wondering aloud. "I'll bet they're hot on your trail."

Joseph explained his situation and present plan to go into hiding until the enemy's attention is diverted. Then he asked if he could introduce his mother and son.

The "Great Bend B&B" agreed to accept its newest guest. Barbara would be welcomed to stay under a fictitious name, Shirley Walton, and her helping with housework and childcare would be a welcome relief for the overworked housewife, Amy, who was giving much more of her time to gardening. She also intended to do canning, the home preservation of fresh fruits and vegetables. Jason had become an enthusiastic hunter. He was learning how to smoke his meats.

Any charge for room and board would be settled upon her final departure, whenever that may be, but the rate would be less than $500 per month, depending on her productivity, a daily rate of less than $17.

Joseph was grateful, but Barbara was reluctant.

After a prolonged goodbye with repeated promise, Barbara accepted her new accommodation with the hope of a new life, and maybe even a new family. Joseph promised to send email messages after Darren suggested that they could use temporary phones. Jason would also get a burner and open a separate account. Her address would be Shirley.Walton051526@gmail.com. Every couple of months Jason would destroy her phone and replace it with a new one. This was a measure he would take for additional safety. They agreed that it was best not to make any phone calls to each other.

Barbara held her son tightly, in a prolonged embrace. "I don't want to lose you again," she said through her tears. "Promise me that you will come back for me."

"I'll never let go," he said in reassurance.

Soon the duo of insurgency leaders passed through Keystone, South Dakota, and it resembled a ghost town more than the mecca of tourism it once was. They continued, through the Black Hills, headed for the Big Horn National Forest in Wyoming. Joseph thought it best to avoid Interstate 90, as they were more likely to encounter trouble there. They quickly refueled in Keystone, while speaking to no one, and boldly sporting their hats and beards.

Minutes thereafter, Darren saw Mount Rushmore off in the distance. The early afternoon sun had already started its course to the west. The eyes of Lincoln were shadowed, displayed as large black ovals. Today, the great presidents seemed melancholic, even mournful.

He remembered visiting there with his grandparents when he was in elementary school. Grandpa Fred sat in silence, reverently, before the national monument. He was awe inspired.

"Old Abe doesn't seem to be happy today," Darren observed thoughtfully.

"Well, maybe seeing his letter published on the internet will lift his spirits somewhat," Joseph suggested.

"But he must be rolling over in his grave," he said after further consideration. "This country is in such a terrible mess."

Darren watched as the monument began to disappear behind encroaching woodlands. Joseph looked to his son as if seeking permission to continue.

"Sometimes, I wonder what God is doing," he offered. "I have seen so much tragedy… so much killing in his name, and in the name of religion."

"President Lincoln also struggled with the question of God's role in it all," Darren suggested. "What did he say? Oh yes, he believed in Divine Providence," and he thought some more. "And in God's sovereignty," he remembered. "Didn't Lincoln say in our letter that we should trust God and remain faithful?"

"Yeah, that's about right," Joseph acknowledged while staring straight ahead. "But there are so many unanswered questions. Sometimes I just wonder."

"For example," he continued, "there are so many contradictions in war."

Darren offered a nod of approval. "They kept me in a safe place. I never really experienced it – except through the eyes of a satellite."

"You were lucky," his father suggested. "I saw it all, and had lots of time to digest its irony."

"With every victory we win, they become stronger and we become weaker."

With a confused look, Darren asked, "what do you mean?"

"They become more determined. We lose resolve, and our resources are depleted."

"Why do they get stronger… really!?" Joseph asked rhetorically, and then answered himself. "Because hatred is *very* strong," and he paused. "Every one of their leaders we kill becomes a martyr, and ten more get in line to take his place."

There was silence in their car as both digested the revelation.

"Here's what I don't understand," Joseph said, "If ISIL isn't true to Islam, than why haven't they disowned the radicals? Why aren't they policing their own ranks? Why aren't Islamic countries also fighting against the terrorism of ISIL?"

"I just haven't been able to make any sense of it all," the weary warrior concluded. "All my life I have stood for religious freedom and opposed islamophobia. But today, after their invasion, it seems obvious that the radical element defines Islam. They just can't have it both ways."

Darren swallowed hard and pondered if he was allowed to ask this callous man a personal question. "Well, you believe in God?" He paused and looked toward his father. "Don't you?"

"Oh, it's more than luck, that's for sure," Joseph answered quickly and smiled. "Some of us in the desert were supposed to live, that's obvious. There's no other explanation for it. One is killed, and the man next to him, still alive… It's a conundrum," and he shifted his eyes to see if his vocabulary had impressed.

"Dad, I don't mean to be disrespectful, but I believe that God is much more than fate," Darren objected, "and religion." He paused for effect. "There were many times when Grandpa Fred talked about God," he offered in reconciliation. "After Cindy died we went to church a lot. I heard their message," Darren continued. "But I think that my grandfather influenced me more than anything else."

"Yes, he was a good man. I sure wish I had had that time with him," the son admitted.

"I believe that we live forever," Darren felt an urgent boldness to share his convictions. "The problem with this world is the evil in it," he declared and paused to see if the talk was still accepted. "The next one will be perfect."

"But how can you be so sure that your religion is the right one," Joseph asked sincerely.

"It's not religion, for me," Darren answered. "God wants reconciliation, a personal relationship with us. Jesus came to pay the price, the penalty we owe for our sin, the offence that separates us. He's the only way to become reconnected with God."

Joseph made no response, so Darren continued.

"And he conquered death with the power of a love greater than anything we can ever comprehend." Darren looked to his father who was nodding slightly. "God's way is sacrificial love. It's the only way to defeat hate," Darren shared from his heart. "Religion doesn't work."

"It's hard for me too," he concluded. "But that's what I want to believe."

The men let the words settle in their midst and in their minds. After what seemed like a prolonged silence, Joseph responded, "I don't deserve it." He was speaking softly. Then after turning to make eye contact, Joseph confessed, "I'm just sorry, for so much of my life."

"I know…" Darren offered in consolation. "It's okay. We have the future to make up for it."

"I can only hope so," Joseph's voice trailed off. "I can only hope so."

SECTION THREE

OUR DESTINY – many are persecuted. Others lured

by the promise of prosperity face the ultimate test and accept the mark. It

defines their destiny.

Mecca, the power that occupied Levant prior to the Crusades of

long ago, establishes a monarch in the U.S. that wars against Christianity

and the remnant of American patriotism. This dictator is known in

prophetic writings as the "Beast." He denies the resurrection of Christ,

and the salvation of His followers, blaspheming against God. He

demands all people to pledge their loyalty to him, in denial of Jesus

Christ. Many true and loyal Christians are executed by the dictator in

defiance of their God, publically mocking the Sovereign.

The Beast quickly rises as a world leader, with global initiatives headquartered in Dubai. Europe unites with Asia. An ancillary government is established in Rome, Vatican City, the former citadel of Christianity. An image of the antichrist is erected in Jerusalem. The whole world marvels at the proliferation of this new order. A united Eurasia begins to flourish. The genocide of Christianity continues.

Wherever the corpse is, there the vultures will gather. The masses of the world venerate their new leaders.

A second, subservient dictator is placed in Rome. He performs miraculous signs to deceive the multitudes and demands that all worship the Beast. He initiates a world monetary system identified by a mark placed on their right hand or forehead. It is the name of the Beast, the number of his name, the number of a man – six hundred, threescore and six.

A microchip here designates the person's citizenship in the new world order. Those who pledge allegiance to it are granted the rations of survival as commerce begins anew with the promise of great prosperity.

But God has issued a warning concerning this affiliation as follows:

"If anyone worships the beast and its image and receives a mark on his forehead or on his hand, he also will drink the wine of God's wrath, poured full strength into the cup of his anger, and he will be tormented with fire and sulfur in the presence of the holy angels and in the presence of the Lamb. And the smoke of their torment goes up forever and ever, and they have no rest, day or night, these worshipers of the beast and its image, and whoever receives the mark of its name.

Here is a call for the endurance of the saints, those who keep the commandments of God and their faith in Jesus." 1

The masses of the new world order are drawn to the glory of Dubai. For some who have come to know Christ, the threat is too great. They accept and pledge themselves to Islam and its promise of communal peace. The churches' organization of religious denominations is dissolved.

Few are watching and waiting for the coming of a warrior from heaven called "Faithful and True".

1: Revelation 14:9-12

Chapter 7

He is sifting out the hearts of men before His judgment-seat,

Muslim officials who occupy the defeated nation act quickly to first establish Islam as the new state religion. They convert public schools into information centers, health clinics, and mosques with prayers held in the gymnasiums. These become local Islamic Centers, under the jurisdiction of regional centers.

Everyone is required to report to their local center within thirty days. There they are injected with a VerifiedID microchip. It has a RFID, Radio Frequency Identification, circuit that allows the person to be scanned and tracked. Each time he or she comes to participate in prayers, his attendance is recorded and registered by the microchip. New Muslims are required to attend on Friday, their holy day, for congregational prayers.

The location of the chip at the time it is installed is determined by the supervising health official. The person's forehead is preferred; however, some are not able to receive it there due to a limitation. The alternate location is the right hand. The placement of the microchip is designated by large Abjad numerals, tattooed on the forehead or right hand. This number is sacred to Muslims and represents the person's submission to the supreme authority of Islam.

After the chip is placed, the new citizen of the UISA recites the pledge of allegiance in front of a camera and enters the new mosque for instruction, prayers, and worship of their god.

A new worldwide system of commerce is initiated using the microchips. Gone are the dollars, euros, pesos, rubles, renminbi, shillings, and pounds. As a person faithful to their district's Sharia enters their mosque, they pause to face a scanner. It registers their attendance and updates their account, verifying and increasing their monetary value for making purchases at stores of all types.

Even in private sales, a barcode is acquired and scanned to represent and document the exchange, adjusting the balances of the parties to the transaction, within the computerized data bank maintained by the new regime.

The U. S. Food and Drug Administration has established standards for an implantable radio frequency transponder system, (RFID chip) that are Class II compliant. These chips are intended to convey patient identification and health information. Other uses are possible as the chip links to an external database and, or GPS.

Deidra ponders political and religious questions as she joins the Muslim society. She wonders about their motivation in invading America and their determination to dominate the world.

The tension between races and religions has existed for nearly 4,000 years. In the Christian Bible the covenant of God continues from Father Abraham to his son Isaac and grandson Jacob. The lineage of their generations until Jesus Christ is recorded.

In other religious assertion, the promise goes from patriarch Abraham to his firstborn son Ishmael, the elder brother of Isaac, and then to Esau, the elder brother of Jacob.

Esau married Malhalath, his first cousin, the daughter of Ishmael, and their generations continue until this day. This union established the ancestry of the Arab nations.

The seeds of estrangement caused by the exile of Ishmael and his mother Hagar resulted in antagonism within the original faith family. It generated a conflict of religious discord that would endure for more than four thousand years. It resulted in many military clashes and climaxed in the domination exercised during these end times.

At its height of power, Islam dominated the Ottoman Empire from 1299 to 1923. History documents its many religious wars.

Deidra is one of the first to receive the microchip and the mark. Now she is very busy, often working long into the night, with sixteen hour shifts. She knows that she is bankrolling more than most people, but experiences little appreciation for her show of dedication. Today she is feeling resentful of the drudgery it has become.

She is conducting the initial interview, entering information required for the initialization of the microchip. Before her is a young woman who appears to be very nervous. She is jittery.

"What is your age?" Deidra asks.

"Eighteen," she answers precisely without the offer of conversation. The girl wears dingy, tattered clothes; her hands are dirty, and her eyes are surrounded by dark circles anchored on small, puffy facial sacks.

"Where are your parents," Deidra redirects.

"Gone… in the disaster."

Deidra looks but quickly turns away, not wanting to be impacted by the despair this girl wears outwardly.

"Are you healthy, need any medications?" this agent for the new Muslim state asks.

Avoiding the question posed, the young woman is suddenly panicked and blurts out, "I'm a Christian. What are you going to do to me?"

Deidra pulls back on her head covering. "Honey, look at me," she demands despite the tattoo on her forehead, "Look at my face."

Tears well up in the young woman's eyes. Her face is contorted. Her entire body begins to shake.

"Look at me!" Deidra demands while raising her voice. "Do I look like an Arab?"

And after a moment's pause, Deidra continues her rant. "I'm American. I grew up just like you, in a Christian family. But that's all gone now."

"No… no! It can't be!" the frightened woman responds in firm conviction.

"Gone, gone for good!" she announces as Deidra hits her desk with a clenched fist. "We are now a new nation. There is only one religion that remains, one system of commerce."

"I can't do it! I won't do it!" she screams and bolts for the door.

An armed guard dressed in a soldier's uniform is watching from his post nearby. Deidra nods to him and he draws a stun gun as he begins his pursuit.

The young woman is quickly apprehended and placed in a van with others who choose dissention. Deidra has heard rumors, but is unsure of their destination, not wanting to know anymore about it. It is referred to as a reeducation camp.

A federal plan to detain large numbers of U.S. citizens deemed to be a threat to national security is reported to have been developed in 1984, known as Rex 84, it is Readiness Exercise 1984.

During a state of national emergency, as declared by the President of the United States, the armed forces are used to roundup those who are considered to be in opposition to the government. The military is authorized to direct the movements of civilian populations at state and regional levels.

In theory, the establishment of reeducation camps, such as those used after the Vietnam War, is authorized, but details of such camps have not been disclosed.

It is reported that following the war, North Vietnam imprisoned up to 300,000 supporters of South Vietnam, the enemy at their southern border. These included former military officers, government workers, and supporters of the former government. Reeducation was implemented in the camps. Prisoners were incarcerated for as long as seventeen years. It is alleged that thousands were tortured or abused.

Operation Garden Plot is a subprogram of Rex 84. It provides a detailed plan for the U.S. Army and National Guard to respond to major domestic civil disturbances. It is under the control of the U.S. Northern Command (NORTHCOM).

It has been months since Darren fled from his apartment in Virginia but today a squadron of armed federal agents are breaking down its door. The Islamic Religious Police, IRP, are hot on his heels. This raid was ordered after Deidra reluctantly provided her fraternal twin's last known address of residence.

Under the weight of a forty pound pack, Darren pauses to take in the view. They've stopped at a lookout point with a view of Cloud Peak, elevation 13,167 feet. The scenery here is breathtaking.

Bighorn National Forest is the oldest government protected forest lands in the U.S. and attracts many tourists each year. This is troublesome to Joseph. Although they have passed only a few other cars while driving through the park, even one nosey neighbor is too many. There are 1.1 million acres of wilderness here, but still, no good place to hide. There are no back roads on which to hide their car. After hiking away from the park road and delving into the interior, they met a young couple on the trail anxious to share experiences and information. Hikers and campers make entries in journals at prominent points, providing information about their encounters while in the forest.

Joseph and Darren need to fit in, in an unobtrusive way. Hikers here are not inconspicuous, but rather notable, a distinction with recognition not suitable for these two fugitives.

Deidra was the topic of conversation for the past day. Joseph had many questions about his daughter. He still has not met her.

"Can I have a moment," Darren suggests while edging the pack's straps off of his shoulders. With a heavy heart, he is thinking about his twin sister. He feels that she is struggling, and may be in trouble. He says a quick prayer for her. He gazes absent mindedly toward the vista, his eyes finding no boundary. Looking out over the vast wooded valley toward the mountains beyond, he senses freedom's call. Gone are the days of their playful childhood full of adventure, hopeful days of puberty as each in their own way sought a footing for the challenges to come, and happy reunions, times of sharing and bonding once again. Today Darren feels mournful, that it is all gone.

He cups his hand around his mouth and calls to his past, "Deidra…" He hears her name echo off a distant edifice of gray colored stone. He calls again, somehow expecting to leap the great expanse between them, thousands of miles. "Deidra," and the haunting reverberation answers in hollow reply. "Deidra, are you in trouble?" he speaks softly this time, hoping to release his concern. But no answer comes for reassurance and his suspicion of harm remains.

The duo continued south on Route 16, through Hazelton which still contains the remnants left by early settlers, including a post office, no longer in operation. Facilities for the park, vacant at the time of their visit, are also located here. They exited Bighorn at its southern border. Joseph is in pursuit of a place that is even more reclusive. Two hours later in a wooded area along Sawmill Creek, off of Hazelton Road, Darren spotted a lane full of weeds. There are no recent tire tracks. Joseph saw it too and slowed the car to a crawl. "What do you think?" he asked. "Maybe we should try it?"

"Might be a cabin in there…" Darren reasoned.

"Yeah, but I hate to make fresh tracks," Joseph countered and thought for a minute."Let's go up a couple of miles and look for a place to stash the car. Then we can hike in."

"Okay," Darren confirmed. "I need a walk and some fresh air."

Soon they came upon a small house with a gravel driveway. The place seemed to be minimally maintained and unoccupied. Joseph pulled in and backed the car alongside the house, in a parking area.

"I don't think anyone is here," Darren observed. "But I'll go and check. Let's be sure."

He stepped onto the front porch with a bang as the floor board twisted under his weight and a dog began barking inside. He could hear it scrambling, sliding and scratching the wood floor in the front room. With a loud thump the Doberman mixed breed jumped against the glass of the front window nearest to the door. Surprised by the charge, Darren retreated backward as he saw the window bulge outward at its seams. The dog was snarling, showing his long pointed teeth and slobbering on the glass that quickly fogged. The sight of the canine's cuspids caused a shot of adrenalin to be released in Darren's brain.

"Shut up, you old fart," a voice was heard within. There were loud footsteps and the sound of a door slammed, and then the one he faced opened and Darren found himself looking at a scruffy old man. He was bearded and unshaven. His dungarees and flannel shirt were worn and showed holes at the protrusion of the knees and elbows. He wore a knit stocking hat, pulled down upon his bushy eyebrows.

"Hey stranger," his greeting seemed friendly. "What can I do you for?"

"Hello, sir," Darren intended respect and submission as he continued, "Sorry to bother you. But we were wondering if we could park our car here."

The old man looked puzzled and scratched at the side of his head, exposing his left ear, full of hair.

"Why ya lookin' to do that?" he asked.

"Oh, we want to set out on foot, hike up into the mountains. Maybe get a raccoon if we're lucky," Darren suggested, searching for a reason that made sense.

"Out of season," he seemed to puff like an old tractor. "But them varmint are a real nuisance. Fine by me if you kill 'em," and he spit onto the porch floor. "Where you at?" he asked.

"Oh, over there," Darren pointed to his car.

"Well don't be blockin' me in. Move it back there, along the shed," he ordered.

"Thanks, I appreciate it," Darren offered.

The old homesteader nodded and spit again.

Darren turned to leave but stalled. He turned back toward his suspicious host. "Oh, I'd like to camp out, maybe for a couple of days. Do you mind?"

"That ain't any of my business."

"Don't worry, I'll be back. I'll need the car to return home," Darren offered in assurance, hoping the old man would not show any interest in it during his absence.

"No concern of mine," he replied. "Hey, you, young fella..." he called back as Darren was about to step off the porch. "In case you get too many of them coons, I could use one," he suggested.

Darren smiled, "I'll see what I can do for you."

Back at the car Joseph looked concerned. He was hoping not to encounter another person in these parts. "Well?" he asked impatiently.

"Old duffer wants it parked by the shed. I think he's okay," Darren offered. "Let's put it in, as far back as we can. If it's out of sight, hopefully, he'll just forget about it. We can come back and move it in a couple of days, when we find a better place."

Soon they had their packs on and with their rifles in hand, set out on foot and walked directly away from the house, not wanting to give the old man a chance to see Joseph.

They hiked back along the mountain ridge to the location of the lane. Sure enough, there was a cabin there in a large clearing. It was a one and one-half story bungalow, with a sleeping loft on the second floor. It had a rusty metal roof. The shed roof on the front porch was leaning to one end, appearing like it might collapse at any moment. One of the front windows was boarded over. The front door had planks nailed diagonally across the opening and a "No Trespassing" sign was tacked there. It was curled and stained from the elements. Its warning had faded with the neglect of years gone by.

At one end of the shack stood a chimney made of cinder blocks, with a rusted stovepipe perched on its top.

"What do you think?" Darren asked and suggested quickly, "looks like there might be a woodstove."

"Perfect!" Joseph affirmed as he walked to the rear of the shack. "Let's see what is inside."

Chapter 8

He hath loosed the fateful lightning of His terrible swift sword,

The message of Lincoln's letter is broadcast far and wide. It is replayed and repeated, again, and again. The annals of patriotic men and women who strove in the time known as The Reconstruction, following the Civil War, echo in the minds and hearts of weary Americans as they begin to unite for rebuilding.

Their ancestors had also suffered great loss, but then spoke words of reconciliation in hope of a new tomorrow. This rich heritage, eloquently stated by the words of America's hero of liberation, is now stirring in the hearts of an increasing number of people. Saving America and preserving their past, is now the purpose of the power in their will.

Like a mighty gale upon the blades of a windmill, the wheel of freedom primed by Lincoln's urging spins once again with increasing velocity.

Their hope is not found in the plan offered by the new occupying force. These people are different. They came from a foreign land. They require loyalty to their god and to their religion. The arrogance of their demands is obvious when contrasted by Lincoln's humble plea.

Patriots of Lincoln's way, liberty, now decreed by a message written by his hand almost 200 years ago, have fallen into bondage, pressed as slaves into a system ordered by a new dictatorial regime, an evil taskmaster, much like the owners of those imported from Africa during the nineteenth century.

And in the vestibules of the mosques and offices of these new rulers in America, their anger is exploding. The insurgency must be contained!

Deidra is working in such an office occupied by other women. They are not allowed to work with men in this new society. In her own way, emboldened by her own determination, Deidra hopes to influence the other women here. Today she has removed her hijab and has tossed it disrespectfully onto her desk. It remains there despite the objection and warning of her co-workers. Deidra is tired of being covered. She misses the experience of beauty: possessing the confidence it grants and feeling pride while displaying it to others.

Suddenly, the door to the room is thrown open and bangs against the wall. Two men dressed in black leap in like prowling panters. Their anger is evident on their bearded faces. Their authority is established by the handguns holstered at their sides. One man points toward Deidra and declares, "There she is."

Deidra stumbles as she stands to address the unexpected intruders. "What, what did I do?" she pleads.

One strong hand grabs her arm above her elbow and shakes her violently. "Why are you not wearing the hijab?! Now you have exposed yourself to me and I will not be responsible for your intrusion upon my righteousness! You are defiling us!" he declares and looks away while still grasping her arm.

When he looks back he sees her standing there defiant in confusion.

"Put it on!" he yells. "Cover yourself! You are in the presence of Muslim men and the IRP!"

"The police?" she questions as she fumbles with her head covering. "Wh, wh, why?" she stammers. "What have I done?"

"You are coming with us. That is enough. No questions," he instructs and yanks on her elbow.

Deidra trips on the base of her office chair and pulls away as she lunges for her purse, now obviously panicked.

"You come now!" he scolds and grabs at her again, this time much firmer.

Outside at the curb she is shoved into the rear of a black Suburban. Sitting there is a higher ranking Muslim official, evident by his calm demeanor and attire. He wears a thobe and checkered keffiyeh. He does not turn his head but stares straight ahead without any acknowledgement of his new passenger. The men who abducted her quickly enter the SUV in front, one to drive.

Deidra peers out of the dark tinted window, wondering where she is being taken and why she is allowed to see the route. They are soon racing on a highway while exiting the city. The mountains of northern Virginia come into view. She is fearful of a desolate place.

Not wanting to offend the man sitting next to her, Deidra does not turn her head toward him or speak to him. After several hours, the car is traversing a narrow road. It slows at what appears to be an entry gate. She shifts her eyes to peripherally see the letters of the sign at the guardhouse. It says, "AHAB." The car lunges downward, drops into an underground parking garage and stops abruptly. The men exit without saying a word. She watches as one opens her door and stands there in silent command.

Deidra is taken into a small room filled with computer monitors. Here is an unusual chair which reminds her of a seat in a 4DX theater.

"Do you know what this is," the man who accosted her at her office asks.

She simply shakes her head negatively.

"It's a ground control station," he informs rudely. "Do you know what they do here?" and he pauses. "Who operated this equipment here?"

She shakes her head again, the same way.

"This is where your brother piloted the drones," he whined. "He killed many of our comrades."

He continued with his questioning, "Where is he now? I need to know where he is right now!"

"You mean Darren," she wheezed softly in response to the inquiry.

"Yes, of course! Where is he?!"

"I don't know," Deidra answered. "I already gave you the address of the last place where he lived."

"Where is he now?!" her captor reiterated loudly.

"I, I don't know," she answered softly as she began to realize the seriousness of the threat she now faced.

"Sit her down. Show her."

A man dressed in black shoved her toward a chair as another member of the IRP began typing on a keyboard. The monitor before her began displaying a YouTube video recording.

She saw a man, a stranger, holding a piece of paper. It was a letter, and he was talking about it. Then he proceeded to read the letter. The camera shifted slightly and another man walked past the recorder into its view and sat down behind the one reading the letter.

She gasped. It was Darren.

After the stranger finished reading the letter and she thought she heard him say something about Abraham Lincoln, Darren picked up an automatic rifle and holding it high in the air called for all American patriots to fight back against the invading radical Muslims.

The monitor went blank.

"Do you know these two men," the question came quickly.

Hanging her head low, Deidra hoped she would not have to answer. A man pulled on her hijab, partially removing the covering and yanking her head back. The number boldly tattooed on her forehead was fully displayed.

"Answer him!"

"Yes, that was my brother. Darren," she admitted reluctantly.

"What about the other man," he persisted, "who is he?"

"I have never seen him before," she said defensively.

"His name is Joseph. Joseph Daniels! You don't know of him?" the question was rephrased.

"No," she answered quickly, but her thoughts were racing. *"Did he say Daniels?"* she pondered. *"Could he be related to me?"*

"Joseph Daniels!!" he shouted in her face, his hot breath upon her forehead and his saliva splashing into her eyes. "You don't know your very own father?!"

Deidra was stunned by his words and looked quickly toward the computer monitor hoping to get another glimpse of the man that was a stranger to her, the father she never met. *"My father? It can't be. This can't really be him?"* her rational mind objected.

The interrogator infuriated by her lack of response grabbed her face and squeezed her chin with a pressure so intense that it hurt her teeth. Her mouth was cut inside and she recognized the taste of blood. "Answer me!" he shouted directly into her face.

Deidra returned her gaze to him and saw the evil of a hatred that was rehearsed and repeated for thousands of years. Fear overwhelmed her. Terror exploded in her brain. There was no escape. She was incapable of a defense. And for the first time in many years, since the day her little sister drowned and she became as hard as steel, she felt tears moisten her cheeks. She began to tremble.

"Get her out of here!" he ordered and shoved her head back hard enough to bang it against the top of the chair. "Give her some time to think about it."

Two men grabbed her and dragged her down a hallway. They opened a steel door and shoved her inside. It was a small room with a ceiling light but no window. There was no furniture. It was 3 PM, the first day of her incarceration.

She was sitting on the floor, leaning into the corner with her knees pulled up to her chest and wrapped in her arms. Her head was resting there when she finally drifted into a restless sleep. Then the door opened and startled her. A hand appeared and tossed a clear plastic bottle onto the floor. It contained 16 ounces of water. It was 6 AM, the second day of confinement.

The day passed slowly with her mind tormented by the haunts of fear. She had no way to keep track of time. She said no prayer but repeated over and over in her mind, *"I am valuable to them, I have to be."* This was the only comfort she could find. Finally, she dozed again.

In the afternoon of her third day jailed as a terrorist, the door popped open and the two men who abducted her reappeared. One reached for her, still sitting on the floor. "Come on. It's your time." And he yanked her to her feet.

The room she was taken to next had a small table and two chairs. Deidra was pushed into one chair and her hands pulled behind it where they were tied together with a nylon zip-tie. Her feet were also fastened together. A man took the seat across the table from her and clicked on a bright light. It was aimed into her face.

The questions of two days prior were posed once again. Deidra pleaded for mercy. "Please, please! I'd tell you where they are, if I only knew."

Finally, a man in formal Muslim attire stepped forward. He had been standing against the wall behind her. She had not seen him there. He grabbed at her head covering and yanked her head back, causing a surge of pain in the back of her neck. The hijab fell to the floor. With his left hand he took a fist full of her long blonde hair and wrapped it around his fingers. As he pulled her head back she could see the black beard hair and stubble under his chin and on his neck. He leaned forward.

"Ms. Daniels. I am a ranking officer, a caliphate. I descend from the Ottoman Dynasty. And I am losing patience with you!"

"No," she pleaded. "I have told you everything I know. Look, I became a Muslim and worked hard for you. What more can I do?"

"Tell the truth," he shouted. "You have already many times missed holy day prayers," he corrected and sighed. Then he drew his revolver, a 9 mm handgun, a Glock 19, and pressed its barrel upon the soft flesh of her forehead. A clicking sound reverberated in her brain like the sound of clashing cymbals. He cocked the trigger.

"You must know something more!" he demanded. He pressed harder extending her neck even farther.

"My grandmother," Deidra suddenly remembered. "She might know."

"What do you mean?" he asked and eased the handgun away slightly. With his left hand he was still pulling on her hair, keeping her head yanked back.

"I got an email from her… asking me to come and visit," Deidra offered.

"Where is this grandmother of yours?"

"I, I don't really know." She looked deep into his black eyes and saw a flicker, the embers of hell.

Her dark blue eyes full of terror still expressed ambition, her desire for life. A square indent on her forehead showed where the gun had been pressed. A black circle within it was marked by the residue of shots recently fired.

"I'll ask you one more time," he warned. "Where is she?"

"Somewhere in Wisconsin. She didn't say."

He yanked on her head and neck again.

"I didn't answer her yet," Deidra explained quickly. "But I can find out," she offered. "I'll get the info for you," she offered pleadingly.

But it was too little, too late.

"Many will die for the holy cause," his words were cold as liquid nitrogen. A pale blue vapor vented from his mouth as he replaced the handgun on her forehead. Holding it there, he took a step back. "You are no longer of any use to us. Americans are like rotten eggs. The essence of life has already left them."

John Parker was the man assigned to be Lincoln's bodyguard, the night the President was assassinated. Parker was supposed to be sitting in the chair that blocked the doorway providing entry to a hallway that led to the upper level state box used by President Abraham Lincoln at Ford's Theater. But Parker heard the call of an alcoholic and left his post to feed his addiction at a tavern next door to the theater. Parker even persuaded Lincoln's

carriage driver, Charles Forbes, to join him at the bar. It was that fateful night of April 14, 1865.

Forbes, feeling the influence of strong drink, left the tavern and went into the theater to sit at the guard's post. Perhaps he was covering for his friend.

The assassin, John Wilkes Booth, knew that Forbes was not trained in law enforcement. He handed a note to him that persuaded him to leave. Booth entered the hallway unencumbered and pulled the derringer from his coat pocket. He quietly pushed open the door to the state box and standing in the shadows cast upon the rear wall he could see the President's head, rising above the back of a rocking chair. The assassin stood just four feet from his intended target. Booth took aim and waited for his cue, a line of script in the play that would generate laughter from the audience.

All the while, Parker, the man responsible for protecting the President was downing a large tankard of ale at Taltavul's Star Saloon.

Even more troubling, history documents that it was already known that Lincoln's bodyguard was undependable.

In 1861 Washington D.C. formed its first Metropolitan Police Department and hired 150 men. Parker took that job after being discharged from the Union army where he served for three months at the beginning of the Civil War. According to published reports, Parker's tenure with the police department was a time of strife for him. Disciplinary charges against Parker included drunk and disorderly conduct. He was acquitted of the charges but because of continuing tensions at the police job, Parker quickly applied for a position as White House bodyguard when it became available. In 1864 the Metropolitan Police began providing men for that service.

And so it was, the President was left exposed, unguarded, by a drunken renegade who showed concern for no one or nothing, except himself, in wanton disregard for others.

The Civil War had just ended, the Confederate army surrendered. The nation shocked was full of hatred. War causalities claimed more than 620,000 men, its patriotic citizens.

Chapter 9

He has sounded forth the trumpet that shall never call retreat,

Splintering wood flies into the air as the door to Deidra's apartment is broken down. Her place is ransacked by the IRP. Minutes later they exit with a pasteboard box containing envelopes, papers, a laptop, and an electronic tablet. Her desktop computer is carried under the arm of one of the officers.

Amy is bent over, pulling weeds in the garden at the Great Bend B&B, host of Barbara Daniels, when she hears tires squeal and stands erect to see two cars racing up the driveway. One is a black SUV, the other a military vehicle, resembling a humvee.

"Jason," she calls. "We have visitors."

He drops his wrench and leans on his right hand to see around the front of his garden tractor from where he is sitting in the grass. His forefinger is bleeding from a slip of a screwdriver, a persistent puncture wound. The tiller attachment has been uncooperative, again.

The day began with brilliant sunshine and the promise of being good, but suddenly dark clouds begin rolling into his psyche as suspicion rises in a howling wind of remorse. His perspective has changed.

Amy takes another look and suddenly feels panicked. She drops her hoe and begins running toward the house. "Barbara," she yells. "Barbara!"

As she gets closer to the porch she sees Barbara standing in the open doorway, a dish towel in her hand and a puzzled look on her face. The girls are climbing on their swing set nearby. "Quick! Get them into the house," she instructs with increasing concern. "Barbara, be quick!"

Jason attempts to maintain a calm demeanor as he walks briskly toward the intruding caravan, knowing it is his responsibility to greet these unwanted visitors. He sucks the blood off of his finger and spits it on the ground. It is still bleeding. He presses it against his sleeve on his left arm.

The cars stop abruptly, sliding on the gravel. Obviously, they are in a hurry. A large plume of dust continues forward over the top of the vehicles and engulfs Jason, standing near the edge of the driveway, between them and his home. His post is like that of a soldier in uniform at the entry of the White House. Feeling inadequate to exercise authority, Jason grimaces at the realization of the threat unfolding before him, an obvious attack on their peaceful tranquility.

Doors slam quickly and four men approach him. Jason already knows who they are. They have been the topic of discussions at meetings held secretly by local insurgents, which he attended with enthusiasm. He has heard of raids nearby in Milwaukee when certain residents were taken.

Thinking about Joseph, he tries to hide his concern and swallows hard. It was just two days ago that Barbara received an email from her son and grandson. It is still in the e-folder on her phone.

"Mr. Michaels, I need to speak with Mrs. Daniels," says the one who is apparently in charge. He offers no identification or explanation. "May I speak with her now?"

Jason notices that the others are resting their hands at their waistline where their weapons are carried, unexposed. "Sorry, I don't know of her," he states boldly. He is unarmed, but they don't know it.

"Michaels, I will demand your full cooperation. You aren't acting foolishly, are you?"

Jason looks at his feet, searching for an answer.

"Michaels, don't resist us or you and your family will suffer the consequences of insurgency. You have one chance to get this right," he warns as he shifts on his feet, taking the stance of a shooter.

"We only have one guest," Jason offers. "Shirley Walton." He looks away hoping to hide his lie and continues, "Do you want to see her?" He clenches his teeth, feeling as a traitor. He could have said she was not home. But he knows they will not be easily put off. He quivers at the thought of them searching his house, intimidating his fragile wife, scaring his little girls.

"I will give you one more chance," the man snarls. "Are you harboring a fugitive?" he suggests participation in a serious crime.

Jason cringes at the thought. "You mean Shirley?" he wheezes.

"Call her to us. Do it now!" is the firm response.

Jason calls to the house, "Shirley, would you please come out here?"

Inside Barbara, Amy, and the girls are huddled together as the women peer out of a window affording them a view of Jason's encounter.

Barbara flushes and begins trembling. She grabs both of Amy's forearms in her hands and pleads, "Amy, I can't go out there. What should we do?"

Thinking quickly she answers, "Barbara, just wait a minute. Maybe they will think you have gone into town or something," and she pulls on her arms to sit her down.

Meanwhile, Jason is beginning to feel their fear while maintaining his post. He kicks at the loose gravel near his right foot and returns his wondering gaze to the man trespassing on his property and home. That man's eyes communicate his evil intent, a message Jason can no longer ignore.

"Barbara," he yells reluctantly. "They know that you're here."

The men watch the rear door of the house for what seems like an hour as time pauses. It opens and Barbara steps out with Amy holding her up, supporting her at her right elbow. After stepping off the porch, Amy releases her and retreats to the safety of the kitchen, within the walls of her fortress.

"Go and get her," their commander orders.

Two men, one on each side of the distraught woman drag her past Jason, still holding his post.

"I'm sorry," he whispers to her, a woman he has come to appreciate, even begin to love.

"I'm really sorry."

"Put her in your vehicle," the command comes quickly.

Jason notices that the officer is staring intently at him and suddenly feels fearful of his next action.

"Don't hesitate next time," he warns. "Let's go," he instructs his men.

"She's welcome to come back," Jason blurts in desperation. "I hope you will bring her back," he suggests.

The commanding officer raises his eyebrows and smirks as if to say, *"Yeah, right."*

It is now the third day since Barbara's interrogation.

Joseph and Darren are feeling gloomy. It has rained all day. They stayed hunkered down in the shack after butchering a deer shot the day before. It is about 8 P.M. and darkness has enveloped them. They are playing cards at their makeshift table, a couple of old crates stacked together. The light of a Coleman lantern flickers on their faces.

"You heard the news?" Joseph asks his son. "A large group of insurgents captured in Colorado. It wasn't pretty."

"What did they do to them?" Darren asks. He studies the cards in his hand, determined to beat his old man, just this once.

"Beheaded the leaders," he notes and declines to further describe their terrible capture. "Publically."

Darren shifts uneasily as he perches himself on the short log he is using as a stool. It is a piece of firewood.

"Bet it's on YouTube," Joseph suggests. "Just like us."

"Bet it's getting more hits than we are," Darren says with regret as he places a card on the crate.

"What was that?" Joseph interrupts his play. "Thought I heard something," and he listens some more. "Better check it out."

Joseph ducks toward the floor and crawls up to the front window that is still uncovered, lifting his head just enough to peer outside. He looks intently into the dark night. Darren knows not to move but to listen earnestly.

"There," he is whispering now. "I heard it too."

Joseph shuffles on his knees as he reaches for his assault rifle. And then he waits. And they wait a little longer.

"I think someone is out there," he breaks the silence, and the sergeant experienced in battle contemplates his next move.

He scurries across the floor to the rear door as Darren grabs for his AR-15 automatic weapon. Joseph looks outside but sees no one.

"I'm headed out," he instructs. "You stay here."

Darren returns a puzzled look. "Then what?"

"I'll circle around, and draw them away," he explains. "When the coast is clear, you can follow in pursuit. We'll catch them in the middle," he commands. But in reality, it is a diversion that he has preconceived, so that his son can escape unharmed. Joseph has anticipated this moment. He is not afraid of a shootout with the enemy.

Their eyes meet and Darren sees a man consumed with purpose asking for permission. Their bond is strong; they are two of a kind. But now there is no time to express feelings, or to say goodbye.

"Good plan," Darren confirms. "Go get 'em."

Now there is a longing in his eyes, the senior man, more aware of the danger they face. He smiles, raises his hand to his forehead and salutes. It is an expression of great respect. "It is an honor to have served with you."

Joseph opens the door and darts into the blackness of night. But they have not perceived the extent of the threat posed against them. The shack is surrounded by more than thirty members of the IRP.

The door hangs open. In the night Darren sees light flickering across the plane, at the tree line. It is a hail of gunfire.

A father has sacrificed himself for his son.

Before he can move there is a smashing sound, the sound of breaking glass ringing in his ears. Darren turns to see thick plumes of gas pouring from a canister that lies on the floor near to him. It is a tear gas grenade.

There is another crashing sound. Incendiary bombs fly in through the open door and rear window. It is a final gun salute, in recognition of his fallen comrade. Flames bust in the air all around him.

A paper floats and shifts in a breeze but still lies on the crate nearby. The corners of the Lincoln letter turn black and curl.

It is incinerated.

But this is just the beginning…

Chapter 10

He is trampling out the vintage where grapes of wrath are stored;

Judgment proclaims truth in light of holy perfection.
It establishes Righteousness Eternal!

Years later, sometime in the future:

A remorseful soul is questioning His judgment, the pronouncement of truth unveiled.

Deidra is this time more of an observer, than a participant. She perceives the excitement of the joy of the redeemed, simultaneously with the dread of knowing that she has not chosen the Lord. There is nothing to numb this painful understanding. This consciousness is raw and hard. It burns as passionate desire.

A resurrected soul is elaborating on her religious affiliations and self-proclaimed accomplishments. "But Lord, we prophesied in your name. I drove out demons. We performed many miracles."

The eyes of the Great Judge flare and fill with fire. His voice echoes at his left side and causes those who had practiced religion for selfish gain to tremble in fear. He raises his left hand and points toward doom. "I never knew you. Away from me, you evildoer!"

And Love does not condemn, but reveals the consequence of choices made by the person and the outcome of the life they lived.

Truth is unmasked and fully revealed.

A long line of people quickly advances toward the Great White Throne. Crystalline light dances before them in brilliant colors. The joyful chorus of the chosen is orchestrated in melodious harmony vastly more beautiful than anything a soul can fully possess. Emotions truly are inadequate, a former dim reflection of the glory known in this resurrected state.

Deidra is followed by Darren, her fraternal twin brother, born only minutes after her arrival on earth. She is thrilled in their momentary reunion even as she is amazed, enthralled in the beauty of the Lord's court.

"Two halves of the same whole – always one." It was their mantra.

She remembers their posing as adorable children, dressed in matching outfits.

"Tied together for all eternity," her mother had said.

But she was wrong!

Now Deidra feels the stabbing truth. It impales her withering heart.

She has denied Christ and now is about to be accountable in a final consequence of retribution for the choices she made during her earthly life.

She failed the ultimate test.

It seems that the clock has stalled. But it is gone, now irrelevant, because time *is* no more. There are no more markers of time, no evidence of its affect, no restarts, and no future hope. Just being. On, and on, and on, and… She advances in the line once again.

There is evidence of the past. Her memory still has a place in this state of being.

She knows of her impending death and eternal damnation, and now she longs to accept and embrace His salvation of healing love. It is fully evident here, in the glorified bodies of those who are adorned and assigned to worship among the multitude of the joyful. They are at His right side. There is nothing she desires more. The momentary pleasures of her physical life are paled before Him.

Others disappear, off to His left, and a few to His right side.

"Please God; oh please forgive me for my selfish life." But she is speaking only to herself. The time of repentance has been delegated to the past age.

She gazes upon the King of Kings. "You are so beautiful... so magnificent, absolutely glorious!! I now see you and understand. I want you more than anything I have ever known before. Please, oh please..."

But the time of grace has concluded. This is the time of accounting, the place of final determination. It is evidence unto confirmation, a judgment decreed by the actions of one's own life.

The awareness of the moment overwhelms her. Her spirit is magnified as her body begins to dissipate, much like the golden leaves that fall off a majestic maple tree with the ultimate arrival of winter. The scenes of her life flash in her mind replaying like the flickering of an old movie projector.

She is entering a spiritual state. The world's disguise is removed. It is unveiled to reveal something hideous. It is a body that will serve her in scorching pain, torture, and torment. It is her eternal being.

As she is summoned to the lake of fire she quickly turns to see her brother, now enthralled in the glory of the King of Kings, the Lord Jesus Christ.

She longs to say goodbye.

But her wailing is unheard by him. It is an initial expression of the pain she will endure henceforth and forever more in her afterlife. Still facing Darren, she is quickly pulled backwards, drawn away like a dead bug in the vacuum of the howling electronic monster that purifies the carpet of the dredges of life. This time all creation is being purged of evil.

This is her ultimate and final goodbye. Two halves of the same whole, they are now separated for all eternity, and although she will know regret as a constant companion, Darren will no longer comprehend the world's striving.

There is no anger or regret on his face. He is consumed in love. It is brilliant light!

The Resurrected Lord welcomes Darren with a warm embrace. As Darren's body is wrapped in His arms, a recreation of his molecules generates warmth within: purifying, healing, and magnifying the spiritual. The deficiencies of the physical are gone. The negatives of the soul are erased. The influences of evil are eradicated.

Darren now lives in the constant Light of the King, replenished daily as he drinks living water from the River of Life. In this new world there is no pain, no loss, no fear, and no regret; but only the joy of true love, ever abounding and increasing all around: constantly brilliant and beautiful light revealing the great mysteries of His creation.

Everything is constantly growing to elaborate the glory of His perfect and beautiful creation in full celebration: light magnificent and music marvelous, all stimulating, and constantly inspiring the spirit to greater heights. This is Darren's eternity; it is life eternal for those redeemed in Jesus Christ.

After Words

To my children:

The Battle Hymn of the Republic defined the cause of tens of thousands of Civil War soldiers who bled and died in the fields of Pennsylvania, our home state. It aroused their spirit unto an eternal perspective. It gave them confidence as they confronted death even as many of them went on to their everlasting home beyond.

My children: hear the words thence decreed to arouse your faith and take heed. Listen with your heart.

Mine eyes have seen the glory of the coming of the Lord;
He is trampling out the vintage where grapes of wrath are stored;
He hath loosed the fateful lightening of His terrible swift sword,
His truth is marching on.

Glory! Glory! Hallelujah!
Glory! Glory! Hallelujah!
Glory! Glory! Hallelujah!
His truth is marching on.

I have seen Him in the watchfires of a hundred circling camps;
They have builded Him an altar in the evening dews and damps;
I can read His righteous sentence by the dim and flaring lamps,
His day is marching on.

Glory! Glory! Hallelujah!
Glory! Glory! Hallelujah!
Glory! Glory! Hallelujah!
His truth is marching on.

I have read a fiery gospel writ in burnish`d rows of steel,
"As ye deal with my contemners, So with you my grace shall deal;"
Let the Hero, born of woman, crush the serpent with his heel,
Since God is marching on.

Glory! Glory! Hallelujah!
Glory! Glory! Hallelujah!
Glory! Glory! Hallelujah!
His truth is marching on.

He has sounded forth the trumpet that shall never call retreat;
He is sifting out the hearts of men before His Judgment Seat.
Oh, be swift, my soul, to answer Him! Be jubilant, my feet!
Our God is marching on.

Glory! Glory! Hallelujah!
Glory! Glory! Hallelujah!
Glory! Glory! Hallelujah!
His truth is marching on.

In the beauty of the lilies Christ was born across the sea,
With a glory in His bosom that transfigures you and me:
As He died to make men holy, let us live to make men free,
While God is marching on.

One of my favorite Christian recording artists, Rich Mullins, stated it this way:

Where are the nails that pierced His hands?
Well the nails have turned to rust
But behold the Man
He is risen
And He reigns
In the hearts of the children
Rising up in His name
Where are the thorns that drew His blood?
Well, the thorns have turned to dust
But not so the love
He has given
No, it remains
In the hearts of the children
Who will love while the nations rage

"The Lord in Heaven laughs,

He knows what is to come.

While all the chiefs of state plan their big attacks,

Against His anointed One."

"The Church of God, she will not bend her knees,

To the gods of this world, though they promise her peace.

She stands her ground,

Stands firm on the Rock.

Watch their walls tumble down when she lives out His love."

(partial lyrics from "While the Nations Rage," by Rich Mullins, 1989: Never Picture Perfect. All credit to Rich Mullins Music, Inc.).

"Be not deceived; God is not mocked: for whatsoever a man soweth, that shall he also reap. For he that soweth to his flesh shall of the flesh reap corruption; but he that soweth to the Spirit shall of the Spirit reap life everlasting." Gal. 6:7-8

Life is a journey – its meaning is found in its destination.

Life is a journey, and up to a certain age we are carried along the pathway. It is easy for the child, despite the hardship their parents endure.

Unaccountability is the child's vehicle. But then he, or she, begins to make choices for himself, herself. It is then that they quickly advance and come to the crossroads. Here is a choice unto good or evil.

The road to the left quickly turns into dirt and becomes like washboard as it goes up a steep hill. It is headed toward the mountain, the sanctuary of God. The journey will be hard. The hiker will trip on stones, stumble on roots, and fall into shallow holes. He will become physically exhausted and mentally distressed. He is often tempted to turn back, to take the easy way, and he may do so.

The weather is extreme on the mountain route. Suffocating heat, freezing cold, driving rain – it constantly makes the next step unstable and uncertain, even treacherous. Satan is visiting here, delivering his torments, fulfilling his **revenge of God**.

The road to the right is wide, smooth and soft to the step, like walking on memory foam. It is lined with shade trees and has benches for the relaxation of its travelers. Near these resting places is a cooler with ice-cold refreshment, convenient and free for the taking. This road goes on a slight downhill grade. It represents an easy walk, even coasting. Most people will choose this route. Yes, they may find conviction along the way. They may think about going back. They may reconsider their destiny – but few will turn around in repentance, even as they become more aware of their affiliations and the consequence of their choices. They are emboldened.

The weather is generally pleasant on this route.

God visits this way to warn the feeble minded and the proud, those living for themselves and consumed in pleasure. He offers Himself in propitiation. He expresses His **repose of confident victory**.

The sojourner to God is attacked with doubt, fear, insecurity, and jealousy as he finds vantage points that allow him to observe the pleasures enjoyed by those headed downhill, going to eternal doom. It looks good. It feels inviting. Perhaps he can temporarily enjoy its immediate comforts. He wonders if he should sample its rewards, even for a short time, and later return to the strenuous climb. Off in the great distance he sees an orange glow mottled by plumes of gray smoke. He hears laughter and the sounds of revelry from those partying below, as they dare each other to be bolder together.

The one headed to hell has little concern of retribution, caught up in the delights of the moment. There are rumors of what is their final destination, warnings of eternal suffering. But those who are gluttons of self gratification laugh them off.

It's not yet known to either pilgrim what soon lies ahead for those on the easy road. There is a cliff from whence they will fall. This is the place of **rebellion**.

Along the journey they have already committed to pleasure, false religion, pride, and self-sufficiency, as demonstrated by Deidra's life.

Some seem to be making little progress. They may even go back and forth. They will not quickly advance to the cliff, but arrive there later in their life. They have heard **Heaven's Repose**, but may ultimately choose **Hell's Revenge**.

Along the way there are many tests, checkpoints for understanding, fostering an awareness of where you are in life, the consequences of your choices, and what you will becme.

Listen carefully. Pay attention to life's lessons. Be aware of denial or indulgence that takes you near to the cliff. It is absolute rebellion or passivity in total self-sufficiency that will push you over the edge. Pause and learn from insightful experiences. Heed conviction

And those who live during end times will face the final and ultimate test. It defines their destiny.

God has explicitly warned against worshiping the beast and receiving the mark. See Revelation 14:9-11.

Enduring souls will find strength from the inspiration of the old hymn possessed by true soldiers.

It will become their "***Battle Hymn of the Faithful.***"

His truth is marching on.

In the beauty of the lilies Christ was born across the sea,
With a glory in His bosom that transfigures you and me:
As He died to make men holy, let us live to make men free,
While God is marching on.

When I was in elementary school my principal, Myron Moss, required that we sing this song in assemblies after reciting the Pledge of Allegiance to the flag. Now, nearly 60 years later, I could never have known the impact of his requirements. I am thankful for godly men who have been uncompromising in speaking conviction into my life. My father, of course, is one of them.

UPDATE: At the time of this writing on November 17, 2016, earthquaketrack.com reports tremors in California measured at a magnitude of 1.5 or greater as follows: 14 earthquakes in the past 24 hours, 147 earthquakes in the past seven days, 589 earthquakes in the past 30 days, and 7,243 earthquakes in the past year.

And finally from Rich Mullins:

There's a comin' of glory,

There's a comin' of wrath,

There's some mighty things comin'

Comin' to pass.

(partial lyrics from "Quoting Deuteronomy to the Devil," by Rich Mullins and Beaker, 1995: Brother's Keeper. All credit to Edward Grant, Inc. and Kid Brothers of St. Frank Publishing and Rich Mullins Music, Inc.)

Updyke writes not just to entertain, but also to teach. Using his unique and differing style, his novels are integrated with informational and challenging text. *CAUTION:* you are about to enter the astute zone.

Updyke writes with a moral (Christian) perspective that has wide appeal to a broad audience, not specific to any religious institution. See his other books on line at UpdykeBooks.com, sample them with his app that allows you to read or listen with your phone, or purchase them at Amazon.com.

The Contemporary Christian

Stay connected to and encouraged by those who are like-minded and kind hearted:

www.facebook.com/groups/thecontemporarychristian .

It's not what we say, but what God has to say that really matters. Here you will be ushered into WORSHIP and lyrics provide an opportunity for MEDITATION (with only one CLICK)!

Updyke notes, "I can't even imagine who might become linked here. Will you join, and invite others who want to give glory to God? This will be a place where we can share thoughts, ideas, and requests that are more intimate to our faith. You are invited to share your discoveries of contemporary Christian music and other links to media experiences here."

OUR APP: (We've got an APP, and it's FREE!)

Stay connected in fellowship with the app from Updyke Books. (http://www.updykebooks.com/apps-stay-connected). Download the app from the link provided here or directly from the Google Play Store or Apple App Store on your phone.

The app provides the link to The Contemporary Christian and books which you can read or listen to on your phone. It also provides the latest entry from Updyke's blog.

The Contemporary Christian Series

"Love Endures Hope Abounds"
Step 1: *SALVATION* - relinquish your control.

Robert Love is searching for a glimmer of hope. Memories of better times have become miserable haunts from his past.
On the ropes emotionally, fate (or was it God?) intervenes and brings him a new friend, a mentor and wise sage of sorts, with provocative insights. His name is John Wright. He becomes Robert's counselor.
A spiritual battle ensues. Everything changes. Ultimately, love endures and he discovers new meaning for his life.
The truths expressed here, simply and clearly demonstrated by real-life experiences, will also inspire you.

"Wonder and Fear"
STEP 2: *WISDOM* - discover your calling.

A pastor is accused. His soul is scorched by the flames of remorse and fear - doubt's fire!
Will faith save him, or will he be consumed by the haunting questions of his past and the present accusation? Wisdom looms in his searching, even as he rejects his calling.
We are all vulnerable. Doubt comes with a simple suggestion and the question that lacks an adequate answer: "why?"
In this book you'll find answers for the difficult questions that have been haunting you.

"**Alive Again** – The way of life that reveals a love greater than your own."
STEP 3: *RESURRECTION* - yield to power consuming.

They've gone crazy! A police report documents a sighting in the town's cemetery. The report goes viral.
It's not sci-fi or fantasy, but a mystery about a modern-day town that gets caught up in the craze, using the metaphor to teach about life. It's an emotional story that demonstrates the bravery of true love in the face of challenging and life changing hardship. The suspense builds until the truth is revealed!
Are you feeling discouraged? You will find inspiration here as you consider how two young people dealt with the tragedy that befell them.

"**Their After Life** – The earth shakes violently and the struggle of their after lives becomes the ultimate test."
STEP 4: *REVELATION* – realize the life chosen.

Caution: we may be living in the eleventh hour. Learn from the fictional lives of the book's main characters, Deidra and Darren Daniels, fraternal twins. Their legacy has debuted in a post apocalyptic world with insights from the American Civil War.
Understand how history has impacted them. Then, the future is predicted as the fictional account moves forward in time.
If you have been intrigued by current events, you will truly appreciate this read.

The Process of Victorious Living:

If you have opened your heart to the love of God as one willing to accept His sovereignty, you must trust Christ as your Savior. He is God's only provision for reconciliation. Salvation, relinquishing your control, is taught in Step 1, entitled "**Love Endures, Hope Abounds**."

Having received Jesus as your Savior, the next step is to purge your mind and will of any false accusation which you have believed against our Heavenly Father. With the realization of how futile self-righteousness is, you should now comprehend your need for a deeper understanding of God. Step 2 is Wisdom: discover your calling. The pathway of wisdom is offered in, "**Wonder and Fear**."

Books one and two tell the fictional story of Robert Love as they teach the principles of faith.

Resurrection is appropriated in Step 3: yield to power consuming. To abide in Christ is to possess the victory over the temptations and tribulations of this life for the purpose of living in the service of the King. Learn to possess resurrection power in, "**Alive Again**."

Step 4, Revelation: realize the life chosen. God's plan is complete and He shares it with those who want to learn. A fictional scenario of the near future has been presented in this book, "**Their After Life**." An understanding of Revelation will cause us to live carefully and expectantly. We must be diligent to prepare the next generation for what is predicted and warn them about worshiping the beast and taking its mark. Although there are many and varied interpretations of The Book of Revelation in the Bible, the warning about "666" is indisputable, and explicitly stated (Revelation 14:9-11).

"The Lord is working all the time to save, bless, and redeem the lives of his sons and daughters with enduring love. His love is more than we can comprehend! His love never ends.

"Write to me: updykebooks@gmail.com ,

God's Richest Blessings to You,"

Alan Updyke

Post Script

Please help spread the word about **"Their After Life."** Word of mouth is still the best way. Share this book with a member of your family – pass it on! Tell your friends that they can sample this book on their phones.

For your convenience, this book is available to read or listen to on your phone, computer, or tablet. Please try it by downloading my app, Updyke Books, available for free at your app store or from my web site, www.UpdykeBooks.com/apps

Please help me plant spiritual seeds. If this book has been meaningful to you, please help spread the word to others via social media. There are two things you can do now as you visit Updyke Books on Facebook. (See us at: www.Facebook.com/UpdykeBooks.)

Please "LIKE" our page to receive our posts.

Please "SHARE" our posts with your friends. This is most important in spreading the news. As you visit my FB page, www.Facebook.com/UpdykeBooks , please remember that a *LIKE* will reach one person but a *SHARE* will reach fifty.

Your review is critically needed for encouraging others to consider reading "**Their After Life**." Please write to me at UpdykeBooks@gmail.com, or better yet, post a review on Amazon.com.

Here is the link to post a review on Amazon, or search "Alan Updyke" on Amazon. CLICK HERE

Use my web site, www.UpdykeBooks.com/share-encourage/ to access excerpts from my books designed to encourage others as you share them on social media.

My blog: www.UpdykeBooks.com/blog

My YouTube channel: Alan Updyke

www.ingramcontent.com/pod-product-compliance
Lightning Source LLC
Chambersburg PA
CBHW060426180626
46817CB00007B/2685